MISFITS

Characters Only A Mother Could Love

LAWRENCE E. MATRICK, M.D.

Misfits: Characters Only a Mother Could Love
Copyright © 2021 by Lawrence Matrick, M.D.
www.lawrencematrick.com

This book is a work of fiction. Names, characters, places, and incidents are either products of the author's imagination or are used fictitiously. Any resemblance to actual persons, living or dead, events or locales is entirely coincidental.

Cover designer and Interior Formatting: Edge of Water Designs, edgeofwater.com

ISBNs:
978-1-77374-088-1 (Paperback)
978-1-77374-089-8 (E-book)

Bellevue Publishing
Vancouver, BC, Canada

DEDICATION

To my wife, Jean, and also to our children: Marilyn, Diana and Michael for their love, encouragement and support while writing this book and for travelling with me on this journey.

ALSO BY DR. LAWRENCE MATRICK:

M.D. Confidential (It's All Very Hush–Hush)

The Madhouse

The Quisling

Road to Recovery: Following Your Motor Vehicle Accident

ACKNOWLEDGEMENTS

With gratitude and appreciation to my editor, Michelle Balfour.

CONTENTS

ALL THE WORLD'S A STAGE by WILLIAM SHAKESPEARE
(from *As You Like It*, spoken by Jaques)

All the world's a stage,
And all the men and women merely players;
They have their exits and their entrances;
And one man in his time plays many parts,
His acts being seven ages. At first the infant,
Mewling and puking in the nurse's arms;
And then the whining school-boy, with his satchel
And shining morning face, creeping like snail
Unwillingly to school. And then the lover,
Sighing like furnace, with a woeful ballad
Made to his mistress' eyebrow. Then a soldier,
Full of strange oaths, and bearded like the pard,
Jealous in honour, sudden and quick in quarrel,
Seeking the bubble reputation
Even in the cannon's mouth. And then the justice,
In fair round belly with good capon lin'd,
With eyes severe and beard of formal cut,
Full of wise saws and modern instances;
And so he plays his part. The sixth age shifts
Into the lean and slipper'd pantaloon,
With spectacles on nose and pouch on side;
His youthful hose, well sav'd, a world too wide
For his shrunk shank; and his big manly voice,
Turning again toward childish treble, pipes
And whistles in his sound. Last scene of all,
That ends this strange eventful history,
Is second childishness and mere oblivion;
Sans teeth, sans eyes, sans taste, sans everything.

INTRODUCTION

I wanted to write this book because of a mother's everlasting love for her son, who was a confirmed arsonist. I had seen Helmut, a young man in his mid-thirties, in my private office as a psychiatrist by request from a judge (his, and all other names and details in this account, have been changed for the sake of anonymity).

The courts wanted a psychiatric opinion on Helmut before sentencing. His lawyer called me and said, "The judge needs an opinion to know if Helmut was psychotic in setting all those fires."

"Sure," I said. "I'll see him. I'll give you an opinion to see if he was delusional with false ideas or hallucinating: that is, hearing voices telling him to set fires."

After seeing Helmut on four separate occasions in my office, the conclusion was that he was a character disorder, and not psychotic; he was rational and cognitively knew what he was doing as a fire-setter.

He was sentenced to two years less a day at the provincial jail, which has since been demolished. I knew that I would see him there, since I had been the prison's part-time consulting psychiatrist for a number of years.

I recommended a prescription for a mild anti-depressant for him, as he was suffering from a depressive disorder. This was after his long-time girlfriend had moved out of his apartment, and after he had pawned her jewelry to get drugs. The prison physician asked me to see him occasionally to monitor his meds.

Following his sentencing, Helmut's lawyer called me again to ask if I would see his parents. "His father is very angry, and his mother is distraught. I don't know how to help them. Could you please see them once?" he pleaded.

I offered them an appointment a week later. The father was, indeed, beside himself with anger at his third-youngest son. He was so intense and overwhelmed that he talked incessantly for the first half hour. I just listened and let him vent.

Helmut's mother, who also just listened, said quietly that she had heard this before. She was a bright lady, with a pronounced German accent. She was clean, neat, obsessive, and fidgeting with the shawl that covered her graying hair. She sat, pensive and fearing to interrupt.

She finally did. "Doctor, I always knew that my youngest was troubled. Never could express himself at home. If he tried to, then he was always shushed up," she said, furtively looking at her husband.

I didn't want to expand further on this family conflict, as the hour was coming to an end and this wasn't a family therapy session. I reassured them both that Helmut had told me that he had learned his lesson. I would see him often at the prison, and he had agreed to follow-up therapy with me and a very good, qualified psychologist when released.

They both felt relieved. The father felt better after ranting, and Helmut's mother was exhausted. She got up to leave. The father followed her out.

Helmut's mother stopped at the door, turned to me and said, "Doctor, please tell my Helmut that whatever he did, and forever long, I would always love him, no matter what."

"Yes, Mrs. Gottlieb. I certainly will," I said.

She hesitated, then took my hand and held it for a few seconds. "Don't forget. Whatever he did, he will always have his mother's love," she repeated and walked out.

This book is about the impact that various character disorders have, not only on the individual affected, but on their family, friends, community, and society in general. The events and characters depicted in this book are fictitious, and any similarity to actual persons, living or dead, is purely coincidental.

These fictional stories of various characters who are mentally ill illustrate the impact on those personal lives, but also on the workplace and our educational and legal systems, causing turmoil for families and disruption for our society.

This book was written because these characters are actually all visible to us in our communities, and yet they are rarely ever talked about on radio or written about in our newspapers. They are all visible to us as we walk the streets, but ignored as we pass by. They are the unseen, and some are the unwashed. Invisible unless they blatantly act out in an antisocial way, cost the taxpayer more money, injure someone, or make a fuss that becomes an annoyance.

Generally, we don't see those who are street sex workers because they only work at night, or we don't talk about the homeless because we quickly pass them by as they sleep in a covered storefront. We are only bothered when they cost us, the taxpayer, or if they are arsonists, thieves, scammers, or drug pushers.

We ignore the strangers unless they are child molesters or there is domestic violence in the neighborhood and a friend needs protection and a safe house. We all turn a blind eye to the hoarders in run-down hotels, left destitute and a potential hazard to others if the fire marshal doesn't close them down.

We rarely ever act as concerned citizens if we read about the racists and the abuse leveled toward those of different cultures or those who face gender challenges.

As a medical doctor and psychiatrist, I wanted to raise awareness of the plight of those individuals who are psychologically disturbed but living in our community. They all need more services available to them, more awareness from our politicians, and more care and attention from the ordinary citizen.

I hope that the reader will become better acquainted by reading about such characters in our society. We all have a responsibility as informed citizens to help those who need more help. These characters are strangers to all of us, and the fiction stories may be stranger than fiction to you, but they are all frank—possibly uncomfortable to read, but hopefully educational.

All the fictitious stories are about Personality Disorders. Such a character disorder is an enduring pattern of inner experience and behavior that deviates markedly from the expectations of the individual's culture, and is pervasive and inflexible. It has an onset in adolescence or early adulthood, becomes chronically unhealthy over time, and leads to distress and impairment.

This book only deals with a relatively small number of character disorders. The reader will quickly become aware that such individuals have problems with cognition: that is, ways of perceiving and interpreting one's self, other people, and events.

They also have difficulty with affectivity: that is in their range, intensity, and lability of emotions and appropriateness of mood. Finally, interpersonal functioning is problematic, as is their impulse control.

This enduring pattern is inflexible and leads to pervasive problems in personal and social areas. It must be professionally diagnosed, perhaps in several consultations, and other observers may be necessary. Culture-related issues must be considered, and character disordered problems must not be the result of some other substance abuse, medication, or head trauma which requires special diagnostic and treatment methods.

Our understanding and treatment of physical illnesses has developed over time, but unfortunately research and treatment of mental illnesses has not had the same benefit. They are now being referred to as "psychological disorders," "stress illness," "emotional dysfunction," and other such inoffensive and innocuous nomenclature in an attempt to hide the words "mental illness."

Mental health issues have risen in prominence not only due to the Covid-19 viral crisis, but also in response to our school systems. Children are now more prone to anxiety, depression, and post-traumatic stress disorders due to family disruption, a history of abuse, and, more recently, gun violence.

Education systems need more safe havens in schools with counselors who can provide psychological therapies for such students who are under stress.

Statistics reveal that just over 40% of Canadians will have some kind of a mental health problem or illness, and many of these will apparently arise while the person is still working. Some common illnesses that affect so many include overwhelming stress in the workplace, anxiety disorders, depression, and post-traumatic stress disorders (PTSD).

THE HISTORY OF
MENTAL ILLNESS

The history of Character Disorders, also referred to as Personality Disorders, reveals that the mentally ill and those who demonstrate a character disorder have always been shunned across societies and throughout history. They have always been with us, and will be for a long time to come.

Such disorders were well-documented by the early Greeks, Romans, and Egyptians thousands of years ago. Those who hallucinated, heard voices, and expressed fear of others (that is, they were delusional), were considered to be very special and have the ability to see into the future. They were revered as extraordinary due to their psychotic manifestations.

Several hundreds of years ago, it was decided that the public had to be protected from such deranged individuals, whether character disorders or the severely mentally ill, but also that they required protection from the abusive public. Thus, they were housed in mental institutions.

The first written knowledge of such intuitions came from the

Arab Islamic states, as explained by travelers to those areas. Cairo had such a hospital in the 9th century for the care of the insane, which employed compassion, support, and music therapy as treatment.

In medieval Europe, the insane were housed in some monasteries, small villages, and in city towers called "fools' towers." The hospital in Paris, Hotel-Dieu, had a few cells in the basement solely for lunatics. Also, the Teutonic Knights had hospitals with small attached "madhouses."

In 1285, a treatise by Sheppard, "Development of Mental Health Law and Practice," described a case of a "frantic and mad" individual due to "the instigation of the devil." Thus, such illness was then associated with Satan.

Spain had many institutions, and in London, England, The Priory of Saint Mary of Bethlehem was built in 1247—later known as the famous Bedlam.

Much later, throughout England and Europe, the parish authorities assisted families both financially and with nursing care for their mentally disabled. Such a parish might further help by housing a mentally ill family member in a private madhouse or board them out with other caring families.

Some charitable institutions, supported by religious groups, were available, such as Bedlam. In the early 18th century, many cities throughout England had private institutions. Unfortunately, there are records of some institutions selling or renting out their patients in the form of slavery. Such individuals served as serfs in various workhouses, mills, and mines. In the early 19th century, the College of Physicians in England put a stop to this practice.

Privately-run asylums developed in the 1600s, and in 1632 the Bethlem Royal Hospital in London recorded that in the lower levels there was "a parlor, a kitchen, larders, and several rooms where distracted people were held." Those who were violent were chained, but all others could roam about and even had access to the public areas close by.

When King George III had a remission of his mental disorder in 1789, such disorders were finally seen to be treatable and curative. Moral and compassionate treatments prevailed with the French physician, Philippe Pinel, in 1792 at the Bicêtre Hospital near Paris. Pinel and others freed patients of chains and dark dungeons were abandoned.

At that time, it was agreed that such illness was the result of social and psychological stress, hereditary tendencies, or the result of physiological damage. Attendants and other nursing personnel were taught to be compassionate, supportive, and humane. Patients were encouraged to work in the hospitals and on discharge were assisted within the public workplace.

In England particularly, cottage-like homes developed to house those requiring less supervision. Such cottages held 50-70 patients. It produced a familial environment, where patients were encouraged to perform chores to allow a sense of contribution. They were rewarded with Christmas, Easter, or other holiday incentives.

I and my wife, a nurse, had the opportunity to work in such humane and modern cottage hospitals at the Runwell Hospital in Wickford, Essex and St. Ebba's Hospital in Epsom, Surrey in the early 1960s. I was surprised that at Easter, Christmas, and other festive occasions the women received a small glass of sherry and the men a small tankard of beer at mealtime. They were light-years ahead of the huge, red-brick, four-story monstrosities in Canada and the United States that held four to five thousand patients.

In the USA, the first psychiatric institution opened in 1773 in Virginia: the Eastern State Hospital. Later, in the early 19th century, many such hospitals opened throughout the States. In Canada, every province had immense, three- to four-story ornate hospitals. Each building was fronted by magnificent Corinthian columns, and some contained grand staircases. However, a few levels had bars on the windows, and many had padded cells.

Each was a community within itself, and in the 1960s they became more civilized with beauty parlors, cafeterias, movie houses, game rooms, private showers on each ward, and overnight sleeping rooms for families from afar who came to visit their relatives.

I myself worked at the Weyburn Mental Hospital in Saskatchewan in the summer of 1951, the Brandon Mental Hospital in Manitoba in 1956, and then at Essondale, later called Riverview, in British Columbia in 1958 and again in 1961 and 1964. I was impressed with the caring, supportive, and considerate attitude of all nursing, medical, and personnel ancillary care.

In the 70s and early 80s, there was an international movement to decentralize such large institutions and move patients into their communities to be with their families. Thus, group homes were established. Patients were encouraged to be treated at home with therapists visiting close by. Outpatient units were attached to every medical facility in the area. However, many patients were unable to adapt, since they had been uneducated, unemployed, and had no training whatsoever.

There has been an outcry by the public, since many such patients have been seen to be on the streets, addicted to drugs and alcohol, and sleeping in storefronts, parks, or alleys. The prisons now house many mentally ill individuals. Housing for the poor, the destitute, the indigent, and the mentally ill is obviously wholly inadequate.

It is important to realize that institutionalized patients before the 1970s were generally very well-cared for. Prior to their hospitalization, many mentally ill were unemployed, uneducated, shunned, isolated, rejected, abused, exploited, or addicted to drugs and alcohol; upon their discharge, many unfortunately returned to their old habits.

With hospitalization, they received good medical attention, proper hygiene, adequate nutrition, and companionship. Many worked in the kitchens, laundry, libraries, and farms, or as gardeners, aides to the mechanics, assistants to the nurses and medical staff, cleaners, barbers, and hair stylists. They formed close, lasting bonds with the staff and with each other, and often had supportive family visitation, occupational therapies, and regular religious spiritual assistance.

Such hospitals often had festive nights with food, music, and even dances, especially during special occasions. Once weekly, a hospital had a movie night held in large auditoriums, and occasionally such patients were entertained by outside groups of performers.

With the "progressive" drive to close such hospitals throughout the world in the 70s, all such patients returned to receive "treatment in the community," and were moved into halfway houses or to be with their families. As to treatment, they saw a counselor, nurse, or a psychiatrist once per month for fifteen minutes to readjust their medication.

These patients remained poorly prepared for life outside of the institution: they were unemployed, shunned, isolated in their communities, and left on social welfare. Many became "the homeless" on the streets: addicted to drugs and alcohol, behaving in antisocial activities, prostitution, and often subsequently suffering imprisonment.

Change requires a large amount of funding for rehabilitation, re-education, close supervision by counselors and therapists, treatment facilities, and better housing. Such change requires greater advocacy, raising the profile of mental illness, and the need for open public discussion by individuals and community groups.

> *"Nobody escapes being wounded. We are all wounded people, whether physically, emotionally, mentally, or spiritually. The main question is not, 'How can we hide our wounds?' so we don't have to be embarrassed, but 'How can we put our woundedness in the service of others?' When our wounds cease to be a source of shame, and become a source of healing, we have become wounded healers."*

– Henri Jozef Machiel Nouwen

GILBERT, THE FIRE-SETTER

Gil, as the few friends that he had called him, had never completed grade ten, never had much of a father around, and never had any close family supports. That is, other than his mother, who had been depressed since Gil's father left but found periodic solace in the strange men coming and going in the house. And in her dependence on the bottle.

Those who met Gil at school laughed at him due to his nervous hyperactivity syndrome, his slight stature, occasional lisp, and the slant in his eyes.

"I could never remember that diagnothis about my nerves, neatly printed out for me, by that therapist on that one-time brief thession that I had with her," he lisped as he told his good and only friend, Anatol, one warm evening in Edmonton.

Gil liked Anatol, who protected Gil from the bullies at school that often pushed or knocked Gil over in fun. Anatol was a big, strong, hirsute guy. He was strange in some ways and quite effeminate in many others. Gil was dependent on him for the drugs he freely provided to his good buddy.

In turn, Anatol was dependent on Gil for the occasional intimate manual favors that Gil provided freely for his good buddy. It was behind Gil's house in the late evenings. After such gratification, almost weekly, they would both set fire to the garbage bins in a nearby park.

It always happened after they left the back of Gil's house, joked about some girls at school, laughed, and smoked some dope. Gil always brought a small jar of gasoline, sprinkled some into the bins, and threw in a match. They both laughed as they heard the fire engines roaring in the distance after the neighbors called.

Anatol was curious about Gil having seen a psychologist that one time. After they watched the flames rise and ran from the park, Gil told Anatol about his experience. They sat and had another toke on a bench.

"I was really impressed by her swanky private office, in a swanky high-rise building. It was arranged for by that judge I was sent to see, all for setting a simple fire in my neighbor's back yard." He giggled, coughed, chewed his wad of gum, and blew smoke out of his nostrils.

"What for? Any cash, buddy?" Anatol asked, interested in making some easy money.

Gil laughed as he put the wad of gum behind his ear, ready for another time. "It was only for ten dollars. Given to me by a neighbor who always complained about the noithe next door," Gilbert lisped.

Anatol listened, laughed along with his buddy, and puffed on his last joint.

As they sat, they quietly exchanged information about their families. Anatol was curious about Gil's eyes. Anatol went first. "My grandfather gave me my name, 'Anatol.' I was born in Ankara—

that's in Turkey, buddy Gil—but been here most of my life. How about you, Gil, my friend?" Anatol asked.

Gil was a bit hesitant. He puffed on his joint and finally came out with it. "My pa came from China, somewhere. Never saw him much. Married my ma when she was just off the reserve: just sixteen, she was. Said my pa had family, kids, back home," he replied. He watched for some reaction as the street lights came on.

Anatol said nothing except, "You have three sisters. I like that middle one, Bertha. Told me she was a year younger than you. Seventeen." He made a rude gesture that Gil didn't like.

Gilbert was downcast as he explained further. "My pa left us when I was a kid. I was sad, deprethed for two years. Felt better when I set fire to that Chinese shrine in the city park. Ha!" He laughed and slapped his thigh.

Anatol said nothing. They got up from the park bench, stomped on the remains of their cigarettes, and left once they saw the police car in the distance.

Anatol ran off into a back lane as Gil saw the police car making its rounds after the fire. He started to run, which was a big mistake. The car stopped and picked Gil up on the street while Anatol hid down the lane. Gil was arrested, charged with arson, and given a short prison sentence for his first offence.

The only education poor, chubby Gilbert had was to learn a trade as a carpenter's mate while he served his short term in prison.

"You are to desist from setting fires, for arson on multiple occasions as recorded by the police but your first charge in this here court," the judge said, looking down at him sternly.

While in prison, he became very depressed; he wasn't allowed to play with matches and set fires as he did when a youngster.

Just before Gilbert went to prison, Anatol reminded his friend.

"Yeah, lighting matches and throwing them at the dogs and cats, building huge bonfires in the public parks at nighttime, and setting fires to garbage cans in our neighborhood. Fun times, buddy."

His mother, a not-so-kindly parent, but a divorced woman now on government assistance, often brought him blueberry scones and candies while in prison. "Gilbert, poor boy; I hope you are receiving an education here, as your father did when he was often in prison." His poor mother cried as she left each time.

Unfortunately, while at the provincial prison, Gilbert received more than just an education in carpentry; much more than he ever bargained for. He was now a young man in his late teens, overweight with long, scraggly, unkempt hair, a face full of acne, and infected scabs on his hands from lighting matches and fire-setting.

While at the correctional service there was not only the physical abuse but also the mental taunting and sexual exploitation from the older inmates. After all, they all needed some form of release while in captivity, and in a variety of forms. Gilbert was their unwilling pawn and patsy, very well-taught by his buddy, Anatol, in the past.

But after all was said and done to him he did receive some compensation with all the perverted abuse. With this variety of abuse, it was like the sexual arousal he'd felt when he told that shrink some time ago, before he went to prison: "It was down there, deep, inthide, in my crotch, at the bonfires that I thecretly planned for days and days, lady," he lisped and laughed, embarrassed.

The lady just sat quietly, wrote in a pad, and listened. Finally she said to her client, "The judge wrote to me, Gilbert, for an opinion. I see that it gave you a sense of power and accomplishment. For the ten dollars you received one day from that older kid, Jimmy down the block, to destroy a brand-new bike. It was the bicycle that 'the big bully owned,' you said. He made fun of you and your lisp, and he 'stupidly left it outside one time.'"

Gilbert roared with glee at the memory, which caused the small bulging mass in his crotch to swell as he reminisced, sitting there. "It happened on a dark thtormy day, late at night. I uthsed my grandfather's propane welding torch on the tires and on the frame of that bike," he lisped. He had walked away and left the therapist's door ajar.

In the prison, poor Gilbert was one of several who uneasily succumbed to groping by the perverts. He was never able to fight back, but somehow he rather enjoyed the warped attention, as perverse as it was. It was that other kind of human warmth that he'd never gotten from his mother, but did from setting fires, often for a few dollars.

Gilbert was also somewhat physically retarded: slow in all his movements, hooked on marijuana and his mother's boyfriend's rye whiskey. This he secreted when they were busy in his mother's bedroom. His eyes twitched with nervousness and his speech faltered. He was also laughed at in prison since he spoke, they said, like Elmer Fudd in the comics: with a bad lisp.

He quickly became the butt of all jokes, referred to as "Elmer" at times, or "the Chink" throughout the correctional center, a minimum-security prison outside of Edmonton, Alberta.

"Gilbert, I hear you always crying yourself to sleep after such mental and physical abuse at the carpentry workshop, or after the sexual probing and groping in the communal showers. I can calm you, dear boy," his kindly cellmate, Vittorio, the older Italian wop, as he was affectionately called, kindly offered Gil.

Good old kindly Vittorio would calm Gilbert at night by cuddling up to him in his bunk bed. Gilbert willingly accepted such a human touch here, there, and everywhere, since the winters were freezing cold in Alberta and the prison was damp.

Vittorio was comforting enough, but it was Gilbert's transistor radio with his tapes and his earphones that put him to sleep. He was consoled by listening to "Ring of Fire" by Johnny Cash. His hottest and best tape was "Set Fire to The Rain," sung by Adele, the lady with that seductive voice that helped him get aroused.

Such music and secreted video tapes in prison made up for his childhood predilection for matches, lighters, bonfires, smoking, and watching videos of firefighters dousing forest fires in California or northern Canada and Australia.

It was not just his despair, but also the anger that overwhelmed him. He told Vittorio one night as they cuddled, "It was after the weekly thowers with those men, pointing and laughing at my obvious lack of my manliness. And my thsparse manhood, as my doctor once told me, when he examined me for a bad nervous rash."

Vittorio only held on to him tightly and reassured Gilbert as he gladly manipulated such deficiency and sparseness.

He had not only suppressed anger but inner rage after the pervert, Monty the Moose, used him privately after the other men left the showers. He was slow, Gilbert was, but he was quick enough, and smart enough, to get Monty's home address as his prison sentence wore on.

Monty the Moose had the reputation of being a pusher of all drugs known to man, and a nightly source of the many women he procured for his friends in the neighborhood. He lived well off the sale of drugs and the monetary gains from the ladies, he was proud to explain.

"All of great financial benefit to me, Gilbert, my friend," he said proudly to Gilbert just before Gilbert was released from prison. "And if you ever need some good hash or a good lay, just call me for some good pussy," he added, laughing.

And Gilbert knew all of that, as he appeared dumb and vacant while he stood nearby. But he listened carefully to the other prisoners, who talked about good old Monty. It was a few days before his release that he modestly took a chance.

"Oh, misther Monty," Gilbert lisped, and wept dramatically, with eyes twitching, as he pulled on his trousers after a shower, "So … I'd just like to visit your plathe for a beer some evening, see one of your kind ladies who could help me with my nervousness: you know, down there. And maybe thmoke some shit with you."

Monty snorted in contempt, but he was only too happy to tell him where he lived. He then received a paltry sum from Gilbert in advance for a toke. After all, he preferred Gilbert to his many prostitutes.

Gilbert cried after the pain of such penetration by Monty, but his tears were a symptom of his suppressed anger and the overwhelming rage that he couldn't talk about.

Vittorio held him close one night as Gilbert told him of his anguish. "I see that you take it out by smashing your fists on the concrete walls of this cell until your knuckles bleed, poor boy," Vittorio said kindly.

"Yeth, that Monty guy and what he does reminds me of the anger I had when my pa left the family, Vittorio. And then my mama left to shack up with the neighbor, a hopped-up drug addict."

Gilbert was too ashamed to tell Vittorio that he'd taken out some of that rage on his poor little Rosie. She was the only girl he'd ever known intimately, who lived across the street.

Back in the prison cell, Vittorio just sat back on the toilet seat and watched his cellmate one evening. Gilbert sucked the blood off his knuckles and spat it at the image of Monty that he had drawn on the wall as he listened to his tape, "Great Balls of Fire" by Jerry Lewis.

He smiled as he fell asleep in Vittorio's arms and silently swore that he would receive retribution one day. Vittorio could hear him laughing in his sleep at the vision in his dreams of great flaming balls of fire sweeping over his mother's boyfriend, and then over Monty's house.

He also always felt relief when he got rid of his aggression by hammering, cutting, and banging nails into the soft, cedar planks in the carpentry shop. His prison guard, called Captain Nemo by the inmates since he only talked about his new fishing boat, "The Argo," often berated him for his shoddy work in the carpentry shop.

"You'll never make a good carpenter, buddy boy," Nemo said, laughing. But he occasionally protected him from men like Monty the Moose. After all, he wanted pudgy little Gil all for himself.

In spite of such abuse, poor uneducated Gil was wise enough and always had a plan down the road. As simple-minded as he was, he nevertheless knew how to get revenge on his perpetrators from an early age.

"I learned my ways in my early teens, ethspecially with the lack of my mother, who preferred her cold, crazy hop-head boyfriend, Jonathan, who often visited us in the evenings," he had told his lady shrink on that one occasion.

As a persistent voyeur in his neighborhood, Gilbert often spied in the neighbor's windows. One night, he saw his mother lying with brutish Jonathan in his neighbor's bedroom on the main floor, drugged up and comatose from cocaine. She often stayed overnight while Gilbert, hungry and depressed, snuggled up in his younger sister's bed in the frigid house.

Jonathan was often off with some older whore after leaving his mother and giving Gilbert a licking for forgetting to wash the dishes and clean the house. Gilbert and his younger sister usually ate cold leftovers for supper, alone on those frosty nights in Edmonton.

Gil's plans worked well back then. In order to get revenge, he had crept around the back and set fire to Jonathan's house one night when his mother was asleep in his bed. "That will teach you'se to use my mamma tho wickedly," he cackled as he watched the firemen douse the flames from behind the thicket across the street. He could feel some arousal down there as he watched and laughed, his anger dissipating.

That time he took his little sister with him behind the thicket. "Come sister Bertha, we will both will watch our mamma and that friggin' Jonathan," he said to Bertha as he put the blanket around her to keep her warm. Both adults, mamma and her pothead, stood outside in their undies, freezing to death in late November as the flames spouted high.

Gil had a similar plan all worked out for Monty just after the warden told Gil that he was free to go on parole.

"Tho … I just need to visit you, Monty to thay hello, have a drink and buy sthome speed or dope from time to time. Maybe thee sthome pussy," he told the Moose as he waved goodbye and laughed secretly to himself.

Monty was only too pleased to give Gilbert his address. "And maybe you can have an overnight stay with me, Gil. Or with one of my best girls," Monty said, leering and waving goodbye.

At that time, the Moose and two of the other perverts didn't know that all their residences would go up in flames, for a small sum of cash, once Gil was released from prison. Gil left the prison, tap dancing and listening to his favorite tune by Billy Joel,

"We Didn't Start the Fire," in the springtime of that next year, in the month of April.

Gilbert also still fumed, and had never forgotten the prison sentence given two years ago by that scrawny woman of a judge. "You're quite small for your age, Gilbert, but now that you're almost an adult I sentence you to two years less a day for your fire-setting history in your neighborhood," Judge O'Shaughnessy said back then, looking over her spectacles at Gilbert, who stood next to his lawyer in the court room.

Gilbert looked up to the balcony. He saw that oaf, Jonathan, smiling and clapping his hands as the judge gave her verdict and the sentence. "So … Thuck you, misther," Gilbert lisped as he stared at the man. He also gave him the finger.

Gilbert turned back to the judge and was just about to tell her to piss off when the judge rapped her gavel and walked out of the court room at the end of the day. Gilbert asked his court-appointed legal aid for the judge's address, but was reprimanded by Ms. Tanya Forchuck, the lawyer.

"Listen up, Gilbert. You'll be locked up for twenty years the next time if you're thinking of torching the judge's house when you get out of prison. Smarten up. Be a good lad, now. Change your ways and get rid of your anger, perhaps by going to the gym for a good workout."

'Gilbert the Goat,' as he was called by his classmates while attending Lord Kitchener high school in Edmonton, was left with friends and neighbors when his mamma again shacked up with Jonathan after the fire. Jonathan hustled prostitutes and trafficked them off on the streets, living off their nightly labors.

Gilbert, meanwhile, stole radios, watches, jewelry, any good china he could find, and all else of value from each and every one of the neighbors he briefly lived with to sell for some dope and some booze.

Gilbert fumed when his mamma's last friend, 'Aunty Ethel,' scolded him. "You'll never amount to anything, Gil, if you continue in your wayward ways," Aunty Ethel complained as the police officer took him away. He had been caught setting fire to Ethel's husband's Toyota. He'd been angry because 'Uncle' Jackson wouldn't drive Gil to McDonald's for a hamburger, where he was going to meet young Rosie for the evening.

"So … she can't be pregnant by me," he muttered angrily to himself as he gleefully poured the gasoline onto the hood of 'Uncle' Jackson's brand-new Toyota. It was parked outside that late night. He added as he watched the car burn, "So … I only did it once, for Christ's sake. With Rosie."

It was soon after that when he met Monty the Moose in the provincial prison. Gilbert kept Monty's address secret until the weather warmed. His best-kept secret was the warden's house.

The $500.00 dollars he got from Captain Nemo to torch the warden's house was mostly given to Rosie to look after their little daughter. Beatrice, Rosie had named her.

"That prick, Warden Smolenski, refused to give me a raise after all my years in service." Nemo swore, shook hands, and secretly gave Gilbert the envelope with the cash, as he said goodbye when Gilbert left prison.

It wasn't long after that in July that Gilbert set his plan for revenge and finished spending some of Nemo's leftover money. The warden was on holiday at his cabin on the lake, fishing. It was there at the lake that he got the news that his house had been torched.

Gilbert did it well that late night; he was proud of himself. But he wasn't the brightest candle on the cake as he walked away from the flames: he had left the gasoline can standing near the maple tree in the warden's back yard.

As he quickly walked down the back lane and watched the flames engulf the old wooden structure, he looked back, slapped his thighs, and laughed heartily. With his excitement he thought of that one night with Rosie.

He slept well, but it was the next day that the police arrested him for arson and murder.

"I didn't know that the warden had let his divorced thister and her two young children to thtay at his house for the weekend that July summer," he told the policeman when he was arrested.

"We have your fingerprints on that can you left. The two young children sleeping upstairs succumbed to the smoke, but their mother was fortunate to escape the flames, Gilbert," the chief of police said as the other officer put the handcuffs on to take him away.

Gilbert's fingerprints were all over the can that he had bought brand-new at Home Depot and filled at the local Esso station.

Rosie often visited Gilbert in the penitentiary after the judgment was made. "Little Beatrice will be a pretty girl, but over twenty-five years old when you get out, Gilbert," Rosie said on the telephone through the prison's glass pane as she blew him a kiss.

"I be looking out to thee her then, Rosie."

Rosie blinked and hemmed and hawed for a minute. "Tell you more, Gilbert. Anatol moved in with me, Gilbert. He's a good one to our little Beatrice. Nice papa to her, he is."

Gilbert could see she was nervous about that. "Good for you and the family, Rosie. Good for our daughter to have a real father," he answered with a smile and a wink.

Rosie relaxed, but she had some more news for Gilbert. "Listen good, Gilbert."

Gilbert put the phone closer to his ear. "What is it, Rosie? Tho, you is pregnant again, Rosie?"

"Naw, Gilbert. Your papa found me. Came back to Canada. Said, he did, that he found Jesus at the church he now goes to. A new man, now, he is. Said to me that he was sorry. You know, like the way he treated you and your mamma."

"No shit? Really. Tho … he said that?"

"Yeah. Said he sought forgiveness from Jesus. For being cruel to you, your mama, and your sisters."

"Really? Tho … my old man said that? To my sisters, and my mama? That he found Jesus?"

"Yep. Said he was sorry. Real sorry. Said he would help me with money to raise our little girl, Beatrice. Till you get out, Gilbert," she said.

He was about to hang up the phone, but she had more to tell. "Your pa, Gilbert. He says more to me about your mama. He says that your mama told him that she always loved you, no matter what," Rosie professed as she looked Gilbert in the eye.

"Loved me? No matter what? She, my mama said that?" Gilbert asked as tears welled up in his eyes.

Rosie nodded as she blew her nose in her sleeve. "Yeah, she told your papa that she always knew what you was up to with those matches and fires, but in spite of those ways she always loved you, no matter what."

Gilbert couldn't contain himself; he turned away in embarrassment as his eyes misted up. "My mama really said that? That she loved me in spite of what I was? What I did?"

"That's what she told your papa, once, time ago," Rosie answered through the phone behind the heavy glass screen. She then slowly walked away.

Gilbert watched Rosie leave as he waved goodbye to her. Tears welled up in his eyes and his nose ran with spittle. The prison guard witnessed the pathetic scene from close by. He put his arm around Gilbert briefly and escorted him back to his cell.

"He really did love me. My old man did, Mithter Lorene. My pa will look after Rosie and Beatrice and Anatol. He said he found Jesus. He's a good man, my pa is. Tho was my mama, who loved me still," he said to the guard, wiping his tears away with his fist and blowing his nose in a tissue.

"Maybe you can go to our chapel services on Sunday, Gilbert. Maybe talk to our prison chaplain about your mother," the guard said kindly as he gave Gilbert another clean tissue.

Gilbert stopped to wipe his eyes again. "You know, ah … I still feel bad, guilt like, to have those two children die in that fire I thet, Mithter Lorene."

"A bit older than your own daughter, they was."

"Yeah, a bit older. Maybe I will thee your chaplain. Maybe he can help me find Jesus altho. Like my pa did."

"Maybe, Gilbert. Just maybe," the guard answered as he opened the cell door for Gilbert.

"You think tho?"

Mr. Lorene put the key in the door to lock it and said, "Sure, Gil. After all, you've got lots of time. Only another twenty-five years left to find him."

ARSONISTS

The word 'arson' is derived from the Anglo-French term *arsun*, or *arsoun* meaning fire, branding, or burn on the skin.

It is difficult to write about the profile of a typical arsonist; not many are identified and arrested or undergo psychiatric examination to enter therapy.

Usually they are males between the ages of sixteen to thirty-five with a past history of an unstable childhood with abuse or neglect; a poor school record; an antisocial, petty crime history; a faulty work record; and a lack of stable, interpersonal relationships. There is always a fascination for fire, a need for money, characteristically low intelligence and possibly a mental disorder or a history of addiction.

There are many histories of arsonists, past and present. Guy Fawkes attempted to blow up the Parliament buildings in London in 1605; most likely for political reasons rather than financial, but a fire would have followed no doubt. It was referred to as

November 5th, Bonfire Night. Effigies of Guy Fawkes are still burned at the stake.

A Seattle man, responsible for at least seventy fires in the 80s and 90s was found guilty and sentenced to ninety-nine years. Historical court records name many who set wildfires in California, causing the deaths of many. All were convicted, and some are still in prison.

According to recent statistics, arsonists set about 25% of all fires in America alone, and it is now the most expensive crime in that country. Property loss is extensive, and arson claims over 700 lives annually. It is one of the most difficult crimes to solve and convict because the evidence is lost in the fire and altered significantly by the arsonist.

Juveniles account for the majority of fires, and there are several motives for this explanation. As with Gilbert in the above fictitious story, excitement is the paramount thrill-seeking emotion. They seek attention and are excited when they read about the stories in the newspapers, knowing that everyone is talking about them. It gives them a sense of power, often an overpowering sexual excitement, and gratification of being in charge.

As the arsonist gets older and more courageous, he graduates from simple dumpster fire-setting to larger, occupied dwellings, as Gilbert demonstrated in the above fiction story.

Many then progress to setting fires to bushes and forests; this may have occurred recently in the American west. Many simply become mischievous and enjoy being vandals. It often starts due to peer pressure or just to have fun, since they lack involvement in other acceptable activities enjoyed by all other adolescents.

Again, as with Gilbert, revenge is a motivation for real or ill-conceived injustice. Gilbert was ridiculed, criticized, laughed at, and sexually exploited. He sought revenge on his perpetrators. Such exploitation may have occurred years ago in their youth, but also may be very recent. Revenge is one of the most common motives for a serial arsonist, together with the financial reward.

Hardened criminals may use arson as a way to conceal their other criminal activities. The fire is set to cover up murder, burglary, auto theft, criminal records, or any other criminal evidence.

Profit and monetary gain is a powerful motivation. This includes insurance fraud, property damage paid for by other individuals, or eliminating consumer competition. There may be other factors for revenge, like being paid to destroy property in order to remodel buildings, or for others to gain employment through the loss.

Arsonists may be employed by other criminals to set fires, or perhaps for themselves to act as terrorists. Such extremists target government buildings, places of worship, abortion clinics, and animal laboratories. Such arsonists may claim responsibility openly to make a statement and draw attention to their cause.

Finally, such fire-setting may be the result of mental illness. Arson may be the result of a delusion (a false belief) that someone or some group is doing or about to do harm to that person. Many arsonists are antisocial personality disorders, also known as psychopaths, or are depressed and set fires to relieve themselves of the depression or internalized anger, as Gilbert demonstrated.

Arsonists can't conform to social norms and are deceitful, impulsive, aggressive, and have a disregard for the safety of others. Finally, they are devoid of guilt and lack any semblance of remorse.

Parents must be aware of children who start playing with matches or fire. They must caution and discourage their children from engaging in 'daredevil' behavior and are noticeably excited while watching fires.

Treatment of arsonists is very problematic. This is due to the inherent and pervasive personality disorder and the lack of close interpersonal relationships. If there is a close relationship, then such a person or family member might encourage therapy.

One of the main areas for therapy may be the courts insisting on treatment, or such treatment being available in the prison system. Outside of such incarceration, there is treatment available through a professional therapist, a psychologist, or a referral to a psychiatrist. A family physician may be the first to offer assistance.

It would be imperative for the physician to fully examine that individual to determine the presence of a mental illness. Such may be chronic depression, PTSD, anxiety, drug addiction, a more serious condition like schizophrenia or bipolar disorder, or a cognitive condition like a brain injury or early Alzheimer's.

If a family member or partner is present, then they would be an adjunct in the treatment process. Individual or group therapy or services of a religious person can be most therapeutic. Medication may be required for any of the mental disorders.

CHARLIE, THE HOARDER

"Hey, Mister Scrooge. For Christ's sake, Charlie. If I told you once, I've told you a thousand times. Get this shit out of our bedroom. I can't get into this frigging room to get into bed anymore," Joanna, Charlie's wife, shouted.

Charlie was in the bathroom, filling the shelves with tissue, toilet paper, paper towels, hand wipes, his mother's old shoes, some ratty slippers, and his mother's set of World Encyclopedias from the 1940s. "Yeah, yeah, sweetie. I heard you. Like, I'll clear a path for you again. Real soon: soon as I finish tidying up here."

"And for Jesus' sake, Charlie, stop smoking that shit or you'll burn this place down with all that tissue around," she yelled again as she walked out to see what her husband was doing.

Joanna left the bedroom and looked in at the mess and sighed. "Jesus, man. Alena, our daughter, can't get into this bathroom to wash and brush her teeth no more. Or even have a bath with all this crap around the floor and stuffed into her tub."

Charlie sat down on the toilet seat after moving his mother's fur jacket and hiking boots off the seat and into the bathtub. He pulled out his pack of cigarettes and lit one.

Joanna quickly took the cigarette away and dropped it in the sink. "Charlie, with all this paper around here you'll burn the place down. Our landlord gave us a warning about all this clutter. He told me that the fire department guys told us to clean this shit up. It's a fire trap, you squirreler you," she yelled, frustrated, and pointed to the litter.

Charlie just blew her a kiss and pulled out another cigarette from the pack. He adored his Joanna. He knew that she was smart, highly educated, and was a part-time high school counselor. Charlie didn't like to be left alone when she was at work, but she earned enough to support Charlie and Alena.

Joanna was not too sure of her feelings for Charlie. She had low self-esteem, was always unsure of herself, and depended on having a man around. "Charlie, I want to tell you. Doctor Matson, the psychiatrist, recommended that I leave you. Said that you'd never change."

Charlie perked up and almost gagged on his cigarette. "I didn't know you was still seeing that shrinker, Joanna. My God, woman."

"Sorry, Charlie. We've been going around together for the past six months, we have. He's good to me," she confessed.

Charlie was shocked, but not surprised. "Well, like, we haven't had sex, intimate like, for over a year. Well, like, I'll be damned: that shrinker. It must be against the law."

Joanna didn't want to go any further with that. "Listen up, Charlie. Maybe you should see that other medical therapist again for your depression and this terrible frigging hoarding habit of yours," Joanna said as she helped Charlie up off the toilet seat.

"That guy was the psychiatrist that our doctor referred me to after the medication didn't help. Like, that shrink said I needed a few shock treatments that might cure me. Listen, Joanna. You know all that stuff. Who ever thought that electric shocks to the head would help anyone? Like, crazy, wasn't it, Joanna?"

Joanna cleaned the sink and threw the soggy cigarette into the toilet bowl. She flushed the toilet. She enjoyed lecturing Charlie and had read about some of that in her counseling books. "Over a hundred years ago, some physicians treated general paresis of the insane, GPI, which was caused by the syphilitic spirochete bacteria, with injections of malaria. The malaria illness produced a very high fever, which then produced a convulsion. It was the convulsion, the seizure, that cured the insanity that the guys suffered from."

"No shit. Like, did that really work?"

"Yep, Charlie, it did. Also, electric eels were used by the early Egyptians to hopefully cure a variety of neurological and mental illnesses. Centuries later, magnets and magnetism deployed on the brain were similarly used, but ineffective. When electricity came into use throughout the world, many physicians employed that current. They shocked musculature and the nervous system to cure such neurological deformities, but with questionable results."

Charlie lit up a fresh fag and listened, but was mainly preoccupied with the trash and junk around him—and that Joanna was now sleeping with her shrinker—and thinking how to organize the hoard.

"But in Italy in the mid-1930s, two Italians, Ugo Cerletti and Lucio Bini, working in Genoa, Milan, and then in Rome, experimented with electric currents in the treatment of various neurological illnesses, but again with very little effect. The manager of an abattoir invited them to help shock pigs and other animals into a coma so that they could be more humanely slaughtered, or to be killed with the use of their electric current. I hate pigs. Dirty and slovenly." Joanna stopped and looked at Charlie, who didn't see the comparison, even though he also described himself thusly.

Joanna moved Charlie over to the sink so that his ashes wouldn't fall all over the papers on the floor where he stood. "They brought an ice tong, connected electric wires to the tongs, and passed a current across the pig's frontal lobes. The pigs had a major convulsion, but woke up, squealed, and ran off. The experiment was a miserable failure."

"Ha. Good for the piggies. Smart asses."

Joanna ignored that. She continued, "Despondent, the two Italians went home. But several days later the light bulb flashed, and they had a brilliant idea that changed the course of mental illness treatment for many decades. They realized that they had produced a convulsion in the pigs. They asked the director of a local insane asylum if they could try their convulsive therapy on some of his patients. He agreed, having nothing to lose, and sent them to the attic where the most depraved and psychotic men were housed."

"Not, like, not like me, sweetie. No way, José."

Joanna wasn't so sure about that, but said nothing. "The two 'therapists' asked two burly assistants to hold down six men as they attached their electrified ice tongs to each patient's frontal lobes. They pushed the button to pass an electric pulse across the frontal lobes, and each patient had an uncontrolled major convulsion. This was repeated several times over the course of a few weeks. At the end of two to three weeks the Italians came back and asked to see the patients again. They were nowhere to be found."

"Good for them. Took off, did they? Smart," Charlie said as he threw the butt into the sink.

"Oh, no; they were discharged. Their families took them home. They were well and healthy, and were needed to work in the vineyards," Joanna explained.

"Wow. Like, they cured those guys?"

"Yes, Charlie. Cured them. Cerletti and Bini were nominated for the Nobel Prize in Neurology, but at that time it was awarded elsewhere. ECT treatment was interrupted by the war, but it was used extensively throughout the world after 1945 and still is. It has been well-recorded that the famous writer, Earnest Hemingway, the pianist and movie actor, Oscar Levant, and TV host Dick Cavet were treated with ECT."

"Maybe good for those guys, but still not good for me, Joanna. Like, no way."

"It's better now, Charlie. Now, an anesthetist is present to give the patient an intravenous sedative and a quick-acting anti-convulsive, such that the only way the convulsion is detected is by a flutter of the eyelids or a twitch of the fingers. Also, the current is now unipolar to reduce any memory defect, which used to be a complication. It is often requested by those who want to return to work promptly and not wait for the slower, anti-depressive medications to take effect."

Once more Charlie went to the sink. He pulled out the soggy cigarette butt and laid it out on the shelf to dry out. "Like … I'll clean out the tub so that Alena can have a bath now. I put my mother's clothes and all the tissues and toilet rolls up there, see?" he said proudly and pointed to the over-stuffed shelves with paper tissue hanging out.

"I told you a thousand times: your mother doesn't need all her belongings anymore. She's in that old folk's home, and will be there till she dies, Charlie. You helped her a lot with her chronic depressions, suicides, and all: hospitalizations, drug addictions, booze-ups, and screwing around with bums. You did it all, you did, but now you're a penny-pincher, keeping all her crap."

Charlie pulled out another cigarette but didn't light it, fearing that Joanna would call the firemen again. "Yeah, well, like, you never know. It's in God's hands now, not mine. We may be able to use all these valuable clothes. You know: her furs and shoes. And Alena could wear them and read the newspapers we saved from fifteen years ago. Lots of good history there, Joanna."

"Bullshit. Alena can look up history on Google. Those furs are moth-eaten already. She's not going to wear all that crap from fifty years ago. And what the hell are you saving toilet tissues for?" she asked as she moved three boxes of newspapers away from the door so that she could get out of the room safely.

Charlie was in a sweat and more anxious now that Joanna was berating him like a child. She pointed a finger at him and reminded him, "It's just like you and your mother again, living together in that house full of crap when I met you."

Charlie stepped back from the threatening finger. "I still love my mother, Joanna. Like, she may come back to live with us, even though I'm a pack rat," he answered wiping a tear away and blowing his nose in his mother's cotton, flowered skirt that was on the floor.

Joanna had had enough of all this crap. She'd had heard the same old despondent memories a thousand times before. She was ready to leave Charlie. Or Charlie would have to leave—with all this junk. And take his old depressive, complaining mother out of the old folk's home and go live with him.

"You're nuts, Charlie. The older you get the more you hoard, and the more you hoard the less room we have. And we have less room because you're a penny-pincher. You need a good shrink. Or another place. Or a good shock to the noggin. Somewhere. But not here in Toronto, with me."

Charlie was sad, but now angry to be rejected as he sucked

on his newly-lit cigarette butt. "Maybe. Like, maybe Mother will come to Vancouver with me. God bless her," he answered blowing smoke out his nostrils, angry like a raging bull.

He agitated about that decision for weeks, since his mother was now in intensive care with double pneumonia and a failing heart. Anxious and indecisive, he procrastinated well into September, drinking more and smoking pot daily, battling with the internal fear of losing his Joanna, who was out for nights on end sleeping with that therapist.

Joanna, and now Alena, couldn't stand his wayward ways. He was depressed, had lost his job as a truck driver, and was not interested in finding other work.

Finally, Joanna took a stand after a few months. "And listen up, I and Alena are fed up with more of that junk that you just collected; it's filled the house with even more clutter, Mister Miser."

He got the message finally. He boxed up his hoard and was ready to take half of it with him to Vancouver and put it in storage. He was more depressed when his mother died in the hospital just before he left.

He was even more depressed when he heard that Joanna had hired a garbage truck and threw out the other half of what was in the house. That had happened while he was in the pub, drinking all day, just before he came to say goodbye to Alena.

He blew them a kiss and jumped into his van with the full trailer that was pulling his precious goods.

At the end of that month when he left Joanna and his daughter he was in his early fifties, and now living in the large, one-bedroom basement suite of his brother's rented house in Vancouver. Lucille, his sister-in-law, was horrified. "I saw you unload that trailer and fill my home with all that litter, Charlie. Christ almighty, man, what the Hell for?"

She felt sorry for Charlie, but Lucille quickly accepted him, since he was her first boyfriend and only lover when they met in her late teens. With her pregnancy at that time, Charlie balked, questioned it, denied being the father, and said, "It's all your fault for not having a condom, Lucille."

He had quickly gone to northern Ontario. "I need some money for school. I got a job, to work in the mines," he said as he left Lucille that year.

And that was when Lucille left town to protect her parents from their potential family shame of her pregnancy. She moved in with Broderick, Charlie's brother, in her second month of pregnancy. Stephanie was born seven months later. Broderick wasn't the brightest candle on the cake, and never could subtract seven months from nine, and just accepted Stephanie as his.

Now, twenty-one years later, Charlie was no longer the dapper, young, athletic, virile buck that he once was. Lucille now saw him to be balding, with a sparse, willowy mustache and a bad limp. He was paunchy, dependent on large, bifocal glasses, and forever sucking on a cheap, smelly, smoldering cigar that dangled from his mouth.

Apart from this disappointment, Lucille's sympathy for Charlie's despair quickly eroded as she watched him move in more stuff that he was hoarding. "Charlie, for God's sake, your mother died. Why are you keeping all her clothes and kitchen utensils?" she asked as his brother, Broderick, who was standing close by, tried to shush her up.

Broderick nudged Lucille away. "It's okay, Lucille. He was like that in his teens: a tightwad, I remember. Unable to throw stuff out. We have lots of room," he said, hopefully.

Lucille wasn't so sure about that. They also had their young, twenty-year old daughter, Stephanie still living with them. A bright young woman, she put on a good front with her suffering from Crohn's disease, a severe bowel disorder. She had been a hospital social worker for the past year.

Often in a panic with her bowels, Stephanie always had trouble getting into the bathroom, which was full of her biological father's boxes full of junk.

However, Broderick was also a collector. "It must run in the family," bright young Stephanie once opined.

Broderick had never formerly married Lucille. When she moved in with him, into a dismal basement rental, he had already stored twenty large boxes of his photography gear. That included thousands of family photos of himself with his brother and mother from his teens.

This hoard of Broderick's included hundreds of old reels of movies they could never watch. This was due to the out-dated equipment that he also had. He explained to all within earshot, "These are priceless antiques and could be worth a fortune someday."

To which bright-eyed Stephanie quipped, "We can hardly wait." She didn't mention his old, smelly athletic gear with stinky underwear and dozens of athletic trophies also scattered here and there, and also in her way.

Lucille loved Broderick since he never bothered her, and she accepted him and all of his paraphernalia ever since he had accepted her with her pregnancy many years ago.

Broderick didn't understand why Lucille started talking about her ovaries one day. He wasn't the brightest, and had never heard of "stage four," so considered it to be some kind of a theatrical production that she had been in.

As time went on, Lucille was more and more confined to her

bedroom with her ovarian cancer. Broderick brought her meals, sedatives, and morphine for her severe pains raging throughout her system.

Their extra bedroom also slowly became uninhabitable, and she always just sighed and told visitors who came to offer their condolences and wish her well, "I guess it's just in the family, and I'm stuck with that part of him and his brother."

She was right about the inherited aspect of hoarding, as she added, "He talks of the boxes stacked high as being a barricade against thieves taking over the house."

As she lay in bed she also wistfully listened to Charlie playing his tapes from the basement suite. She got to like the repetitive, "A Song for Mama" by Boyz II Men and would hum along with it as she thought of better days with that stud, Charlie. "Always Be My Baby" by Mariah Carey became one of her favorites.

Stephanie became more depressed with her mother so ill. She received more and more sympathy from Charlie, and she went to visit him more and more in his basement unit. She slept on Charlie's cot full of his mother's clothing. She often never came back up until the late morning hours to bathe and feed her ever-increasingly wasted mother.

Lucille was often up early and always heard Stephanie creeping back up from Charlie's unit to get back into her own bed. Lucille didn't mind and never said anything. She was just so happy to see Stephanie when she brought breakfast to Lucille.

However, Lucille was at the end of her rope when she had trouble maneuvering her wheelchair into her kitchen, bathroom, and living room. By now, Charlie had stuffed much of his mother's boxes upstairs; he'd run out of room downstairs. There was just a narrow aisle available to her to maneuver herself, sometimes using a cane, through the mess. In her own house.

The crises for all four occurred when the owner of the house came to fix a toilet leak. He was overwhelmed with what he saw.

"This is no good, no good," the Russian landlord reiterated. He sternly added after repairing the toilet and was about to leave, "Lucille, you are living in a fire trap. Nyet. No good. Nyet. We will have to do something about this," Boris barked in his thick, Russian accent.

Broderick did nothing about Boris' threat. Lucille was often bed-ridden and couldn't do much about it. But Boris did. He asked the local fire department to examine his house as a potential fire risk.

The fire chief, Captain Richmond, knocked on the door a few days later. In order to open the door fully, he had to forcibly push aside the boxes of athletic gear, albums of old photos, and rusted old bicycles. As he maneuvered himself through the rooms, following a narrow aisle of boxes piled high from room to room, he snapped pictures of the clutter and confusion.

"Your landlord was worried, missus, about a fire. Let's go downstairs and check your suite out, Lucille. Your brother-in law is living there, I'm told," the captain said with a worried look. Lucille was too weak and asked Stephanie to show the captain around the house.

The captain wasn't able to walk down the stairs to the unit below. It was chock-full, on the landing and on every step, with cardboard boxes, stuffed paper bags, and blankets neatly tied together with rope but stuffed with God knew what.

He closed the door as Stephanie silently escorted him around to the back of the house with the back door of the suite. "My uncle was careful to have good access to his unit with this back door, Captain," she said sheepishly.

Captain Richmond continued to take pictures. Charlie had lost his job, since he was too obsessive with details and could never finish one task in any one day. The captain had Charlie stand next to all his personal and beloved belongings. Charlie gladly did so as he puffed on his smoldering cigar, allowing flaming bits of ash to drip down onto the newspaper-laden floor.

Stephanie had come close to Charlie and offered him an ashtray, which he accepted. She lovingly put her arm around Charlie and stood next to him, smiling. "You too: smile, Charlie," the captain said as he snapped a photo of the two with boxes piled high behind them.

Stephanie moved some boxes out of the way as she escorted the captain to the door. "Captain. Can you send me a copy of that nice photo, please?" The captain nodded and sent a digital copy directly to her iPhone.

The captain left, but explained that the house would be shut down as a severe fire hazard. "You all have two weeks to vacate," he said as he handed Stephanie a copy and tacked the original notice to the front door.

Charlie ignored Stephanie's concern as he turned on his iPhone, relit his cigar, and listened to Celine Dion's tune about parenthood, "Because You Loved Me."

At the end of the two weeks, Lucille had succumbed to her ovarian cancer. It was a short but solemn funeral at the local chapel, attended by a few friends and the immediate family. The next day, Charlie was away looking for another rental. He had hired a large van that sadly sat, laden with junk, in the driveway.

Broderick was in total despair as he sat crying in their cluttered bedroom listening to one of Kenny Roger's most popular tunes, "You picked a fine time to leave me Lucille."

Stephanie was the only one with her wits about her as she began cleaning the house of garbage. Charlie said goodbye to Broderick as Stephanie packed her small suitcase and came to Broderick.

She kissed her father on the forehead and explained, "I have a room with my girlfriend, Dorothea, across town, Dad. We both have work in the hospital, and I want to finish my degree in psychology. Charlie will drive me to my new digs: clean and tidy, with no junk all over the place."

"Psychology? Whatever for, Steph?" her father asked with doubt in his voice.

"Well, maybe, just maybe, I can help other pack rats like good old Uncle Charlie, there," she replied, pointing to Charlie, who was leaving the exit door to his unit.

Charlie waved and walked out carrying his last pile of precious junk. He hooked up the trailer to his van. He started up the engine and waited as Stephanie opened the passenger door and slid in next to Charlie.

"My dear uncle, on my mother's side, has an old mansion up the mountain. He lives alone, Stephanie, and said we can move in with him if you like."

"That's very nice of him, Charlie. I will, as it will be cheaper for me to live with you. I hope he has a lot of empty rooms," she said. She didn't mention the back trailer full of stuff and junk.

"Empty rooms? Yes. That's why I called him."

HOARDERS

Charlie, the hoarder in the previous fictitious chapter, was often called Scrooge, miser, tightwad, cheapskate, penny-pincher and a packrat, among other things. All such labels aptly describe such character disorders: basically they are obsessive-compulsive in personality and have a strong family history of hoarding.

The first signs, often in early adolescence, are a build-up of clutter and an inability to throw things away that are not needed. Such are the compulsive, uncontrollable, habitual aspects of the hoarder. Symptoms also include acquiring items despite a lack of space, indecisiveness, procrastination, and avoidance of the obvious.

The exact causes are possibly related to genetics, an obsessive-compulsive personality, and an inability to manage stress factors in one's life. There is some perverse, inherent need for ownership, a strange control over their possessions, plus over-sentimentality for the past.

There is especially a need to remind oneself of one or the other parent, who was most likely a hoarder in the past: as Charlie was thus still attached to his mother through her belongings.

Charlie was prone to maintain and document his past personal family history by retaining such items from long ago. There is a need to preserve the past, hold on to the memory of loved ones, deal with feelings of isolation, and avoid hurting the feelings of the personal family effects hoarded. Finally, it is a way of dealing with stress or to fill the space in the house in such a way that intruders can be kept out.

This disorder has many minor issues applicable to most people. Many are closet clutterers or "pack rats." Even such "minor issues" as the hoarder tells everyone, can interfere with cleaning, cooking, and sleeping, since disorder and confusion are everywhere.

Thus, in summary:

1. It was estimated in a sampling selection by psychologists in 2017 that approximately 4.5 – 5 million Americans are affected by hoarding.
2. Compulsive hoarding has a strong resemblance to obsessive-compulsive disorder, but only that strong similarity. Hoarders may not have that specific personality disorder, but do have some of the characteristics.
3. There is evidence, in an OCD Collaborative Genetics Study, that a strong genetic component to hoarding is present in the family history.
4. It often starts during childhood or in the early teens, but doesn't usually become a problem until adulthood, and especially in a marriage or live-in situation.
5. Hoarding can be more about a fear of throwing something

away, as with Charlie, than about saving. Thinking of throwing something away may precipitate enormous fear. Thus hanging on prevents or reduces anxiety, depression, or other such mental problems.

6. Many hoarders are simply perfectionists, which is a strong component of the obsessive-compulsive character. They fear making the wrong decision and so they keep absolutely everything.

7. Hoarding often runs in families and may accompany mental health problems like depression, social anxiety, or other more severe disorders. Such an individual can often identify a family member with such a problem or with a mental health issue.

8. Compulsive hoarders rarely recognize that they have a problem. Usually, the problem is identified only after the hoarding becomes a problem with other family members or the fire department. The problem may be identified, discussed, or corrected by a mental health worker who is called in.

9. Finally, some hoarders feel that they are protecting their home from potential intruders by making entrance or movement in the home impossible to navigate or to manage a theft.

Treatment of hoarding is difficult unless the hoarder accepts the possibility or is encouraged to seek therapy by family members, friends, the fire department, or a community agency. Even then, they are most reluctant since they do not recognize the hoarding as a disorder.

Therapy is available with a qualified psychologist with cognitive therapy, group therapy, family therapy, counseling through a church minister or other religious affiliation, or the family physician.

A referral to a psychiatrist may be necessary to treat the hoarder with medication and to ascertain if other mental health issues are in evidence. There are excellent medications available, like anti-depressants or tranquillizers, under the direction of that psychiatrist.

The hoarder must remain, for some length of time, in any of the above suggested modalities of therapy and be compliant to treatments. A family member can also be involved in the process for a better prognosis—that is, recovery.

ELSA AND HER EVER-ACHING BODY

"What was her name again, Jasmine?" Dr. Harold Hobson asked on his office phone. "Elsa something? Aha, hold on. Jody, my nurse, just told me. Last name with a 'ski' at the end? I remember seeing her several years ago, Jaz."

Jasmine, the busy, referring family physician was in a hurry, but patiently replied, "Yes, you did, Harold. As a gynecologist you couldn't find anything wrong with her abdomen or pelvis and suggested a referral to a psychiatrist."

Dr. Hobson had just checked Elsa's name on his office laptop that late morning as he talked to Jasmine, the family doctor who referred many patients to him as an obstetrician-gynecologist. He just put in 'Elsa M … ski …' and up came Elsa Metziblonski's profile.

"Yep. Got her full history and examination here, Jaz. She wanted a hysterectomy for her chronic pelvic pains. Very insistent on it. Saw her a few times. Never could find any pathology after all kinds of tests. MRI and ultrasounds. Nothing but a small cyst on her cervix. Excised it. Healthy lady, Jaz. What now?"

"I have all of your reports. I did as you suggested, and Doctor

Clauson, the psychiatrist I refer to, saw her several times. Concluded she was a hysteric: neurotic, unhappy marriage … she wanted to go back to Europe. Told him the doctors were better there."

Hobson smirked, but kept that opinion to himself. "Good for her. So what now, Jaz?"

"She left her husband. Had a hysterectomy in Warsaw. Remarried to a wealthy baron of some kind, but complains of painful intercourse. She liked you and wanted to see you again, Harold. Will you, please? Don't know what to do with her. Lots of aches and sad complaints."

"Yep, Jaz, it all sounds familiar. Thousands of women had hysterectomies for neurotic, hysterical symptoms. Doctors concluded hundreds of years ago that the womb, the *hyster*, in Latin, wandered about the body and caused them to be neurotic and histrionic. The last hysterectomy done for that was in the late fifties in America."

"Really? Will you see her, Harold?" Jasmine pleaded, frustrated. She was in a hurry and didn't need a historical sermon on hysterics or on hysterectomies. She was busy and didn't need a psych lecture. "By the way, she changed her name again. Now is Petra and last name changed to Malborne. She won't use the baron's name yet, she told me."

Dr. Hobson saw the patient that week after she called the office three times, crying with urgent complaints. She came in, weeping, while sitting in the waiting room full of other patients. One lady came to her and held her hand in sympathy.

Hobson's nurse quickly ushered her in to the doctor's office. "I tell you, Doctor, that my husband, the baron … he is demanding of me, down there too much, you know what I mean?" she wailed, jabbing at her lower pelvic area as she quickly sat down in Hobson's office and lifted her skirt.

Hobson listened to her long, pathetic complaints and took a

detailed history of her severe pains during intercourse. She refused a gynecological examination by him and left when he denied immediate surgery as she demanded, refusing to see him further.

After she left, still demanding surgery, he phoned the referring physician, since he thought she should be admitted for a more complete examination with tests and close observation, but not immediate surgery.

"I'll send you a full consultation, Jasmine. I'm worried about her. However, after reassuring her that I'd be gentle she balked and refused the pelvic examination in the presence of my receptionist. She again started to cry hysterically—but no tears, Jaz. Strange."

Jasmine wasn't in a rush this time and was munching on her lunch at her desk. "Yes. Cries a lot. With abdominal pains, she tells me. So, does she have severe vaginismus? Her husband, the Polish baron, came with her when I saw her, and he was beside himself. Told me, in halting English, that she has refused him since the day after their marriage. Too painful, she kept complaining. No pelvic examination, you said?"

"Sorry, Jaz, but I was not able to. When she refused, I assured her that my nurse would be with me during the complete examination. But no way."

"You sound frustrated, Harold. Don't be. She recoiled with me also when I attempted a pelvic examination. She often now brings her 5-year-old daughter, Donna Marie, for me to examine. Says that Donna Marie has hip problems. Kid looks good to me. Nice girl. I checked her over."

"Yep. Would not let me examine her. Just cried and wailed very dramatically. Then, just as quickly she whipped out her iPad and showed me all the statistics on vaginismus and painful intercourse."

"Yes. That's it. Drama queen in my examining room also.

Wouldn't get up on the table in spite of my nurse's reassurance that I wouldn't hurt her. Is her husband beating her?"

"Domestic violence? No evidence of that."

"Hell no, I agree. No evidence of that either when he came separately one time. The baron is a nice, gentle, older gent. Very sympathetic to her complaints, and wants her to have the finest medical care. Said he would send her to the Mayo Clinic. Wants her to see the best, Harold," Jasmine replied as she poured herself a cup of tea.

"That would be pricey, Jaz. Maybe refer her back to the psychiatrist—or maybe she would go as an in-patient under your care for a full work up."

"I thought of that some time ago, but she refused hospitalization. Unless I send her for surgery, as she has insisted often."

"Surgery? What for?"

Jasmine finished her tea. "Wants abdominal surgery. For pains in her lower right abdomen, Harold. Wants an x-ray for Donna Marie's shoulder, also."

"She never told me that."

Jasmine continued, "Complains of constipation and intermittent diarrhea. Vomits sometimes. The baron told me he saw her putting her fingers down her throat … you know, to vomit. When I checked her lower abdomen, fully clothed, she screamed, but I could touch her anywhere and she would scream. I guess I should admit her and do a full work up. Check her for blood in her stool and an ultra sound. Maybe an MRI."

"Good luck," he advised, said goodbye, and hung up.

Jasmine and Harold didn't see their patient again for several months after that. It was the baron who came to see the family doctor when he was referred to a cardiologist by Jasmine for coronary issues. Jasmine saw the baron for follow-up therapy.

"Look, Harold. I'm at my rope's end. Petra wants to see you again. Remember her?" she asked on the phone a few days after her examination of the baron. "She's depressed because her baron is ready to return to Warsaw and take Donna Marie with him. When he came to see me he said that she was told in Frisco by a physician that she needs ovarian surgery."

"She went to Frisco? I thought he was going to send her to the Mayo clinic? Is the little girl his?"

"Yep, he did, but then she went to Frisco. And San Diego, and Mexico City. Then to Boston and New Orleans. No, Donna Marie is hers from her first husband, but the little girl loves the baron."

"Good for the baron. The girl is vulnerable to her mother's need for surgery and must be protected. Ouch; must have cost the baron a bundle, being in the States."

Jasmine excused herself as she talked to her nurse for a minute about an appointment for another patient. When she returned, she said, "It did. All private consults and surgeries. Seven hundred and fifty thousand, all in US funds."

"What the Hell? What kind of surgeries? Jaz?"

"I got copies of all her medical reports. She had a huge volume in her carry-on bag. Took me two days to filter through them. Her left knee was repaired. Tonsils out. Right hip scoped. Right retina in her eye lasered for a fissure in Boston. Surgeon in Mexico City did an abdominal laparotomy; nothing found. Kidney, right side removed for a cyst in New Orleans; it was benign."

"Wow. She must have been in the hospital for months." Harold sighed as he again reviewed the cost in dollars throughout private American clinics. He put Jaz on speakerphone as he lit up a cigarette and opened the window to air the place out.

"She was," Jaz replied, and added, "the gynecologist in Frisco concluded that her pains in her lower left abdomen must be an ovarian tumor. Wrote that she showed him her complaints on her iPad. Oh, she changed her last name again. Now it's Manzoni."

"Wow. Sounds Italian. No longer Polish or Hungarian? So why didn't he operate?"

"It was a she; she was a woman. Petra wouldn't see a male doctor. Said that she didn't trust men to see her privates. The doc was going to admit her, but the baron saw the light bulb go on and got wise to her. He said he was running low of cash and would have to sell his stocks and real estate if she continued. He brought her home."

"Good for him. What happened to the daughter?"

"Petra was taking her to all kinds of pediatricians for abdominal pains. Told all the doctors that Donna Marie had acute appendicitis and needed surgery. The baron is talking about moving out and taking the girl with him."

"Good for him. So now she wants to see me? For surgery?" He waved the smoke out of his window. He was ready to close up and go home, but was still curious about Petra. "Don't send me her reports; I can't see her. She has to be a hysteric, probably a Munchausen syndrome, Jaz, and the poor daughter is now a Munchausen by proxy: that is, the mother is living through her daughter's ailments."

"I agree, and the daughter needs protection. So what do we do, Harold? We've got to help her."

Harold was thinking fast—he wanted to go home. He butted out his cigarette in the ashtray. "You must be firm with her, Jaz. I guess she changes her name often so that the doctors and hospitals don't reject her as a woman constantly seeking attention whenever they pull up her past history. Poor Donna Marie. Now she is her mother's proxy—that is, her mother is getting attention through her daughter's fictionalized medical problems."

Jasmine was also tired at the end of that day. She sighed. "I'll be firm. She must see that psychiatrist again, and if the baron can't manage the girl, then I'll take legal action to protect Donna Marie."

"Yes, do so for the girl, but also get a psych for Petra before she succumbs to an infection or serious surgical complications that could be fatal," Harold replied as he said goodbye and hung up the phone.

It was again a few months later that Jasmine called Harold to refer another patient. "Sure, I'll see Bertha soon, Jaz. Sounds urgent with the Pap smear that you did. Needs quick attention."

"By the way, did you hear about Ms. Elsa … or was it Petra? Bad news, Harold. Like you said could happen."

Harold hesitated, for he feared that Jaz wanted him to see Elsa again. "What's going on?"

"The baron wrote me from Europe. He's in Monaco gambling with another lady who's loaded."

"Lucky guy."

"Yep, but Elsa was not as lucky. He said that she ended up in Taiwan and had abdominal laparotomy urgently for acute pain. Kept showing the doctors there her iPad with all her symptoms. Poor lady succumbed to post-op infection and died soon after."

Harold wasn't surprised, but was sympathetic as he replied, "Ouch, sorry to hear, Jaz. Sorry for the baron, too. Elsa died from complications and infection just like the fictitious story of the Baron Munchausen did long time ago."

"You said that could happen. Tragic, but we all did as much as we could for her. Her daughter is with the baron."

Harold was ready to hang up but remembered to ask, "And

Donna Marie? What happened to that nice kid?"

Jaz sighed audibly but smiled to herself as she answered, "The baron phoned me in gratitude and has the girl with him. Lost a load of cash at the tables, but he married Marissa, a wealthy babe from Monaco, he said."

"Not so lucky at the crap tables but maybe lucky in love, Jaz. Quite a nice story and ending. He also said that Marissa doesn't complain of vaginismus, painful intercourse like Petra did."

"Great. Good thing they were able to join up together, in more ways than one."

"There's more. Apparently Marissa lost her husband and her young son in a fatal car accident a year prior. She adores Donna Marie and says that her prayers were answered, as the good Lord sent the baron and the girl to Monaco to be with her."

MUNCHAUSEN SYNDROME

This syndrome is basically a factitious disorder as detailed in the Manual of Mental disorders. It simply means a strange character disorder that is faked, fraudulent, deceptive, misleading, or a sham. It is imposed on one's self and produced to seek medical attention for the individual. It is often referred to as Munchausen Syndrome, or when that person takes in someone else for treatment, such as a child, it is called by proxy.

Basically it is a falsification of physical or psychological symptoms, or even induction of injury or disease, associated with blatant identified deception. Thus, as with Elsa in the above fictitious story, the individual presents themselves to others as ill, impaired, or injured.

This deceptive behavior is evident even in the absence of obvious external rewards, like the need for money. Occasionally, that person will take their child or some other dependent in for multiple examinations and surgeries or treat the child themselves with medicines, herbals, or other therapies. Such therapies could become fatal.

There are multiple examples of this disorder online and in the press. Some have horrific tales of parents treating their own children in order to achieve prominence and sympathy from friends, doctors, and nurses.

It is a common diagnosis in private billing data in some countries. It is more prevalent in certain cultures where psychological factors are dismissed, poverty is problematic, and health services are inadequate.

At times, Elsa introduced her daughter to various physicians for intensive therapy. This becomes a falsification of illness and is called a Factitious Disorder by Proxy, where the parent or caregiver seeks exceptional attention through those who are under their care.

This disorder by proxy is basically a rare condition. But in such cases, the parent or caregiver may simply lie about symptoms, alter tests (by contaminating a urine sample, for instance), or through poisoning, starving, or causing infection in their child.

In our society, with the advent of the internet and the profusion of information online and in the press, there are a few individuals who may suffer from some form of this type of syndrome. Those who are quite anxious, fearful of some minor malady like a skin disorder, stomach, or breathing problem, will seek clarification online and then seek medical attention.

Such medical information will only enhance their anxieties, and they will then take such concerns to their doctor. They will insist on a diagnosis and treatment despite all reassurance and they will keep moving from medical clinic to medical clinic.

Unfortunately, they may then seek a diagnosis from pseudoprofessionals who will continue to offer "therapy" for a prolonged period. This may often lead to detrimental and physically- or mentally-damaging results.

People with this syndrome deliberately produce and exaggerate their physical symptoms. They may simply lie about their problems or fake their complaints to get attention. The presentation will always be dramatic, but inconsistent.

If they are accepted for treatment by a therapist, then their symptoms may become more severe. It becomes more problematic with frequent admissions, which then lead to predictable relapses in order to gain attention.

Those with this condition also have an extensive knowledge of hospitals, often referring to diagnoses made by other physicians in other cities or countries. Their textbook and internet descriptions are profuse and very well dramatized.

Upon examination they may have multiple surgical scars. New or additional symptoms are produced following negative testing by the physician. They will demand further tests, operations, or other extensive procedures if rejected.

On careful examination, which should include an extensive history, they are found to have had numerous hospital and clinic admissions, and meetings with other doctors or paramedical staff.

Finally, they refuse or are most reluctant to have their physician meet or talk to family, friends, prior doctors, or have previous medical charts available for examination.

Treatment is very difficult because of their movement from physician to physician. However, if they do agree to therapy, then such is available with cognitive behavior treatment with a qualified psychologist.

A referral to a psychiatrist may be necessary for ongoing

psychotherapy. Additional treatment with appropriate medication may be most therapeutic.

Involving the family or friends may add to a better prognosis with individual or group therapy. Additional and concurrent treatment may be found in the person's spiritual or religious community.

SIDNEY, THE PERPETRATOR

Sidney came right into his wife's face as she entered through the entrance door of their condo building. "Kamiko, for Christ's sake, where did you go for two hours?"

Kamiko closed the door behind her. "Oh, just for a walk and some shops, Sidney. Just to look around and get some groceries," she answered, hoping for a smile or at least a kiss on the cheek.

"I told you that one hour was plenty to shop, didn't I? Shopping again, stupid?" Sidney spat out at his wife, almost flooding her face with his saliva.

Kamiko nodded sheepishly and wiped her face in her sleeve as they walked down the hallway to unit 105. She walked past her husband and parked the grocery bag in the kitchen of their small apartment. She was very apprehensive as she pulled her silk scarf over the fading bruise on the right side of her neck.

"Oh, my God, sorry, Daddy. We needed a few groceries, and I had to get some new stockings for the party next door tonight. I'm really looking forward to meeting Suzanne's parents again. They are so sweet, honey," she replied with a nervous tick in her eye.

She was more anxious, chewing gum to placate herself, and she started to scratch at the glowing red rash on her cheek. Sidney was furious, with his face turning crimson and his hands clenched. She'd seen these signs before and feared what was coming.

Sidney had followed Kamiko into the kitchen, and she could see that he was angry at her for being late again and spending his money, which only he controlled.

She tried to divert her husband's attention by petting little Sparky, her small, Scottish terrier puppy who ran into the kitchen after her. "Come on Sparky, let mother give you some water," she cooed.

As Sparky lapped up the water in the kitchen bowl she whispered, "There, there, Sparky, good dog. Mummy has a nice dog bone for you." She reached into her grocery bag and gave her pup the "Crunchy Tidbit" made by Alpoo.

Sparky whirled about, chewing on the small treat in his mouth as he chased his tail around in circles. Kamiko squealed in glee but recoiled when Sidney suddenly gave Sparky a swift boot in the belly.

The pup yelped as he was forcibly kicked against the wall. The pup slunk out of the kitchen with his tail between his legs.

"I told you a million times to keep that mutt out of my kitchen, Kamiko," Sidney shouted and gave Kamiko a wallop on the back, into her right kidney.

Kamiko staggered from the blow and massaged her tender back, just above her backside. She walked away from her husband but opened the bag of groceries to put the milk in the fridge.

"Jesus, Kamiko. I told you not to buy this horse shit again. We don't need ketchup. I don't use that crap." He exploded and threw the bottle into the garbage tin, but then asked, "And did you use that credit card?"

Kamiko's face turned crimson and her rash became more troublesome as she backed away. "Well, yes, Daddy. Oh my God, sweetie, I ran out of cash from the last time," she said defensively, swallowing her gum in terror.

Sidney came right up to her and put his left hand ever-so-gently onto her right shoulder. "Don't call me 'sweetie.' I've got a headache. Besides, I told you again and again that if you need money, then just ask me. I'll give you what you need," he said. He slowly squeezed her shoulder and then moved his left hand closer to the right side of her neck.

Kamiko tried to take his hand away, but he slapped it with his right hand and tightened his left thumb into her neck, where her bruise had just began to fade from his last wallop.

His third wife in five years, Kamiko, was much younger than he, almost adolescent, and of Japanese heritage. He knew that some women of her culture were taught to be obedient and compliant; Sidney liked that in all his women. But to his despair his first two wives drank heavily to calm themselves, sought police protection, a safe house, and then a divorce.

Kamiko tried to calm herself and placate her husband. "Honey, we should visit your father in Kamloops; he is all alone now, poor man. We can take him a present for his coming birthday."

"Oh, just hush up. I'm busy, and we have no time to visit. The football games are all on during the weekends."

Sidney kept his family history to himself, fearing ridicule or sympathy. He kept it to himself that he, his mother, and two older sisters were the victims of their father's physical abuse until his mother had finally left with the children.

With her neck tender again from Sidney's sharp fingernails, Kamiko did hush up. She turned away sharply, scratched at her face, and sat down on the kitchen chair. She slowly moved it behind the table for protection.

She had taken her new package of stockings from the bag on the kitchen table and was ready to try them on. "I'm so sorry about your headache, Sidney. I'll remember to ask you for money the next time I go for the groceries," she said as she looked up to him and tried to smile.

Kamiko stretched her legs out for Sidney to see. "Do you like my new stockings? They will go nicely with that dress I wore when we last went out last year. Oh, my God, I'm really looking forward to Suzanne's party tonight, Sidney."

Sidney glowered. He came to her and snatched the pair out of her hands. He rolled them up and threw them into the garbage tin, next to the bottle of ketchup. "Piss on that. They don't suit you at all. Next time I'll go with you to shop, and I'll pick some nice color for you. Ecru. That color goes better with your skin tone."

Kamiko just nodded obediently. "Suzanne said not to bring presents for her birthday. Just to come for a drink. Maybe we can bring a nice bottle of wine, honey."

Sidney softened and came back to her and kissed her on the cheek. He forced a smile as he tried to speak more kindly. "Look, I told you that I've got a headache. We'll just stay home. I want to watch the football game, Kamiko; the Eagles are playing. We can watch it together, nice and cozy." he leered and grabbed at her breast.

Kamiko turned away from the peck on the cheek and moved his hand away, knowing what he was after. She hesitated. "Suzanne and her husband are so sweet to invite us. You just keep me at home, Sidney, to watch football or baseball games."

"Saves us money."

She hesitated again, but wanted to give her husband some

good news. "For a minute there I thought I was pregnant, love. My period was a few days late, but just started."

"Shit, Kamiko. You're not up to having kids. You couldn't manage a child. I told you. Anyway, those condoms are foolproof," he said with a snicker.

"Oh. But you don't always put them on, Sidney. My mother in Osaka said she'd love some grandchildren," she said, hopefully.

"Your mother couldn't manage you or your little brother. We don't want her meddling with our kids when the time is right. And anyway, you couldn't cope. You've got me to look after, so you better stop visiting her in Japan when she sends you the money," he said, smirking.

"Oh, my God, I do, Sidney. I do look after you. I also had my parrot, Goldilocks to care for, Sidney, until you opened the window and threw her out in the cold of winter."

"That squawker kept chirping and talking while I watched football. A bloody nuisance, just like you are when I'm watching my games: chewing your gum and smacking your lips. Besides, she'll fly south to warm weather."

Kamiko backed off again and put the new wad of gum that she was chewing in the wastebasket. She twisted her back gently to relieve the spasm after the smack to her kidney. "Suzanne told me that her husband heard me crying when you hit me on my neck two weeks ago."

"Spying on us again, was he?"

"No. He was outside gardening and said he was thinking of calling the police, Sidney. Two weeks ago, when I was crying." She added quietly, "Suzanne said that the bruise is fading now, when I paid her a visit yesterday."

"Piss on Walesa, that Hungarian creep. He calls the cops, and

I'll give him what for. You hear? I have a loaded piece here in the kitchen table drawer, just in case he interferes. I'll pistol-whip that bastard."

Kamiko had seen the pistol before, when he had brandished it in her face once and threatened to whip her with it last month. That time was because she had refused to indulge in one of his quirky sex routines. Getting tied up to the bedpost was too painful and humiliating for her.

She was about to leave the kitchen and find her little dog when Sidney grabbed her by the arm and twisted it back. "You stay away from those two neighbors, you hear me?"

"They're the only good friends that I have, Sidney," she replied as she tried to break free. "My God, they are nice people, Sidney," she added, hoping that he would understand.

"I'll find some other nice friends for you, you hear? You leave that up to your good husband," he shouted and threw a towel off the kitchen table at her head.

Kamiko broke into tears as the towel struck her eyes. "Walesa said that your second wife left and went to a safe house after you struck her, but good. That was just before we met. I didn't know that sweetie."

Sidney smirked and pointed a threatening finger at Kamiko. "Yeah, well, she didn't listen to me. That Walesa is a red Commie, a socialist pinko, and a liar. I'll do the same with you as I did to get that no-good woman of mine to listen to her good husband. If you don't listen to me, you hear? Are you deaf, also?" he shouted and came right into her face.

Kamiko tried to back off, as she could see that he was becoming sexually aroused with his aggressive stance as hostility, and rage swept over him. She was aware of his past sexual behavior and knew from past experience what he wanted from her.

He always became aroused after such angry outbursts. She was ready to go to the bathroom partly to be safe but also to empty her full bladder.

As she passed Sidney he grabbed her by the shoulders from behind and swept his hands roughly over her breasts. She recoiled when she heard Sidney demand, "Come, let's have a quickie here on the kitchen table. You'll like us having a go at it right here, and then you can make dinner for your fantastic lover."

Kamiko became tearful and pleaded, "No, Sidney. Not now. I've just started my period and bleeding. It's very tender now for me," she begged, but to no avail. Sidney had already pushed her forcibly and lifted her onto the kitchen table.

He became more livid as she resisted. He swept some dishes and cutlery off the table as she wept in fear. Sidney looked up to see the window open, but he was in a rush to complete what he had started and left it ajar.

Kamiko tried to push him off and locked her legs tight in protection.

Sidney slapped her hard across the face. He forced her legs apart and tore her panties off. "You like it rough, don't you. Well, you're going to get it and like it." He laughed as he punched her again in the head and put his hands around her throat. He laughed and repeated those words as he forced himself into her.

Kamiko cried as he held her throat with one hand and wailed with the pelvic pain as it enveloped her body. As Sidney finished and pulled himself away from her he took her panties and cleaned the menstrual blood off himself with the liner there.

He threw the panties at her and demanded, "Wipe that blood away, bitch, and make me supper, now. Or you'll get what for again."

"Okay, Sidney. I will. I will," she replied in fear. She found her panties on the floor and cleaned the blood off her legs.

She continued to weep as she heard him demand, "And cook good. Not that salmon roll and miso slop you gave me last night. You can't do anything right."

Sidney went to the open window and saw Walesa standing close by on his lawn.

Walesa put his garden rake down and shouted, "Kamiko, are you all right? You were screaming. Suzanne called the police, Kamiko. They will help you."

Kamiko pulled her skirt down and went to the door to tell Walesa that she was all right. She was too late. Sidney, in a seething rage, took his gun from the table drawer and rushed out the door to confront Walesa.

Sidney left the door ajar, and the little dog rushed out to see what was happening. He started to yap and bark at Walesa as Kamiko tried to catch him and hold him back. All that commotion got Sidney more excited, even more so when he saw Walesa raise his garden rake to ward off the pup.

Kamiko was pleading with Sidney, "Please, come back in, sweetie. Walesa didn't mean nothing," she yelled and tried to hold him back, but she was too late. Walesa stood his ground.

He raised the rake in protection as Sidney came at him and pointed the revolver at him. Kamiko yelled out to Suzanne, who came out to help. "Pull your husband away, Suzanne. Take him into the house."

Suzanne stopped, fearing Sidney's wrath and the pistol now pointed at them both. They heard the police siren wailing close by.

Sidney was frothing at the mouth and was ready to take aim. Spittle flowed down his chin.

Kamiko was still imploring, "Don't, Sidney. The police will be here soon." She ran out in front of Walesa, hoping to ward Sidney away.

Sidney, in a frenzy and out of control, fired a shot in Walesa's direction. But Kamiko was in front of Walesa, trying to push him away. The bullet struck Kamiko in the left side of her back. It struck her heart, which exploded deep inside her chest.

Suzanne came to Walesa as she saw Kamiko fall in a heap to the ground, dead. She pulled her husband away just as the police cruiser came to a screeching stop in front of Sidney's house.

Walesa went to Kamiko and tried to lift her inert body off the lawn as Suzanne fell beside Kamiko and wept at the tragic scene.

The policeman driving the car rushed out. The other policeman had his gun drawn and shouted at Sidney, "Drop that gun, mister, or I'll have to shoot. We've been her before to protect your wife."

Sidney obeyed and just dropped his revolver and put his hands up.

Suzanne pulled Walesa away from Kamiko as the other police officer put handcuffs on Sidney. They walked him away to the cruiser. Suzanne, crying and holding onto her husband, called the ambulance on her mobile.

Sidney stopped at the police car door, looked back at Walesa, and shouted for all to hear, "It's all her fault. That stupid woman, my wife, told me to shoot because he threatened me with that rake. It was her fault to get in the way."

The officer told him to be quiet.

"It was all her fault, and I shot in self-defense; stupid woman." Sidney yelled out to the neighbors who came out onto the street. "All her fault," he again shouted.

Sidney was pushed into the back seat of the cruiser. The ambulance turned off its siren and stopped behind the police car.

The neighbors, friends to Kamiko who had come out onto the street, watched in horror.

The policeman explained the situation to the paramedic as Suzanne, still trembling, helped Walesa and the paramedic put the body on the stretcher.

They heard Sidney still shouting in the cruiser, "All her fault; her fault, you heard me?"

DOMESTIC ABUSE AND PERPETRATORS

Perpetrators of domestic violence are those who individually and systematically abuse another to gain power or control in a domestic or intimate relationship. They all carry out harmful, illegal, or immoral acts and come from different backgrounds: some have a personality disorder, and many have difficult upbringings.

In the above fiction story, we only had a glimmer of the perpetrator, Sidney's, past family and childhood history. Such behavior, in all abusers, may be learned through observation during childhood, or in themselves being the victims. They, in turn, may resort to the role of being the abuser and never realize the pain they cause, as in Kamiko's unfortunate case.

Domestic violence can come in a variety of forms, not only physical. Men may be more physically aggressive, but women may be just as hurtful with verbal criticism and emotional or psychological abuse.

There are many examples of domestic violence in the press with the perpetrators being convicted and going to jail. Phil Hartman, the star of Saturday Night Live, was murdered by his wife, Brynn. She confessed and then shot herself. Tina Turner stated in her autobiography, *I, Tina*, that she was severely abused. Her husband, Ike, admitted that it was factual. He died after their separation.

Alcohol, drugs, or serious mental issues may be a factor throughout the history of abuse. However, abusers may have a strong learned or inherited belief that they must be the dominant ones in a relationship and have complete control, as Sidney demonstrated in the above fictionalized story. The control may be emotional, sexual, economic, or physical, and they refuse insight, psychological help, or any form of hopeful communication from their partner.

Unfortunately, the victim themselves often allow the abuse to continue, for some inherent pathological reason in itself. In the example of the above story there was emotional, verbal, and psychological abuse, but also financial or economic manipulation. Kamiko was subjected to cultural abuse in Sidney's scorn of her background. Sexual and physical abuse are of paramount concern and separation, law enforcement, and a safe house are often mandatory to save the victim.

Unfortunately, the victim often remains in the relationship because they believe the abuser, who may plead with them, "It wasn't really me; it was the drink and the drugs." Or, "You made me do it, and I didn't mean it because I just lost control that one time." And, "I won't do it again."

Abuse of and violence against men is not uncommon, and may be regarded as a silent or hidden crime. Men rarely complain, talk about it to others, attempt to resolve the issue with the partner, or inform the appropriate authorities. They fear being referred to as unmanly or weak.

If domestic violence against a man by a woman turns fatal, often the perpetrator is viewed to have been mentally ill during that time. In such a case, the public often has sympathy for the perpetrator. The past history of domestic violence is rarely publicized, since men don't often complain and again, any such violence or abuse is viewed as a mental health issue rather than as a crime.

Domestic abuse and violence may be verbal, emotional, financial, or outright physical. Such examples are kicking, punching, slapping, or biting. Purposefully scalding, burning, throwing objects, and public humiliation and ridicule is common. Finally, threatening to take the children away or turning them against the other spouse, and instituting lengthy court disputes with added threats of financial ruin, is not uncommon.

Treatment of domestic violence and abuse is very difficult as most people are reluctant to complain or admit such behavior to friends, family, or to the proper authorities. They are ashamed to make it public or are coerced by their partner to desist from any such discussion lest there be further retribution by the perpetrator.

The victim usually refuses or is most reluctant to meet with the family physician or any counselor if encouraged to do so. Nor are they willing to meet or talk to family or friends in order to understand the history better.

However, if the partners do agree to therapy, then such is available with cognitive behavior treatment with a qualified psychologist or a family physician. Such therapy can be on an individual basis, in group therapy, or in combined relationship therapy.

A referral to a psychiatrist may be necessary to understand if a mental issue is indeed at work. The victim or perpetrator could benefit from ongoing psychotherapy with a psychiatrist. Additional treatment with the appropriate medication may be most therapeutic.

Involving the family or friends may add to a better prognosis with individual or group therapy. Such concerned friends or interested and supporting family would add to a better prognosis. Additional and concurrent treatment may be found in the person's spiritual or religious community.

JUSTINE, A KLEPTOMANIAC

Justine was about to graduate from high school next month, together with her very wealthy classmate, Rosalina. They were exceptionally good friends, and Justine was very fond of Rosalina. She took care to support her, since Rosalina occasionally received unwelcome remarks from other friends and the neighbors.

Such hostile criticism was due to Rosalina's parents, who still had a strong Italian accent. They were always eating spicy pasta, and Rosalina and her parents were often called "the Wops who lived in the stinky house full of garlic."

Rosalina tried to shrug off the "Wop" remarks and the blatant prejudiced sneers, but Justine could feel her sorrow. Nevertheless, Rosalina was very generous to Justine with clothes and jewelry, since Rosalina could have whatever she wanted whenever she wanted. She often shared such finery with Justine as a friendly payment for her support.

One Monday morning before school, Justine was severely berated by her strict but loving father for coming home so late after a party with Rosalina on Saturday.

"Listen, young lady: coming home just before two in the morning like this past weekend is not to happen again."

And to add insult to injury, he had made a disparaging remark about Rosalina's Italian heritage and family wealth. Justine, as usual, kept her disappointment about such bias bottled up, as she usually did.

Apart from that anger, she was also very despondent. She had confided in her mother the previous day, "Yes, mother, I did feel sad. You were right. It's because the boy I liked, Bart, only paid attention to Rosalina at her house party. It was for Bart's birthday, and he totally avoided me."

Her mother could sense her despair, and put her arm around her daughter in comfort. "Justine, you are prettier than that girl and smarter in your studies at school," she replied, but she was concerned about her daughter's sadness and internalized anxiety.

Justine didn't tell her mother that the two marihuana joints that she'd had that night at the party hadn't calmed her down that much. Nor did the bottle of white wine, which she had brought as a gift for Bart, but drank while Rosalina was on the couch with Bart, causing her to fume even more.

"You're not to be out with that Bartholomew boy so late again, Justine," her mother yelled at her that Monday morning as she dressed for school. "He's not good for you. I could also smell that pot smoke on your clothes when you came in late," she added.

At school Justine was depressed, but also angry at Bart and now more so at Rosalina. She couldn't concentrate on the English essay on Shakespeare her teacher was droning on and on about. She was tense, her stomach gurgled with nausea, she had an anxious, racing heartbeat.

She knew from past emotional experience that her symptoms

were due to her parent's hostile and demeaning attitude and Rosalina kissing Bart on the couch.

She fidgeted while in class. Angry and agitated, she looked at the new silver pen on Rosalina's desktop across the aisle from her. "She won't miss that pen," she muttered to herself as Rosalina left her desk to talk to the teacher about her essay on Shakespeare's *Hamlet*.

Justine looked about as the class emptied. She loved that silver-plated, ballpoint pen with the gold clip on the side. She already had three. "But this one is special," she said quietly to herself. She picked it up, put it in her pocket, and left for the day with the rest of the class.

Justine ignored her good friend who complained on the school steps that someone had stolen her good pen.

Justine just shrugged, prepared to walk home by herself. "Damn thieves. Sorry, Rosalina. Look, I'm in a rush to get home. I'll have to skip the coffee shop with you today," she said as she walked away in a huff, still thinking of Rosalina's lipstick on Bart's cheek at that party.

As she walked home, she took Rosalina's pen out of her pocket and clicked it open and closed it a few times. She could feel her breathing become more regular and her heart rate grow steady. She spat on the pen and threw it into the hedge bordering the sidewalk close to her home.

"Aha, my stomach is suddenly at ease and I'm no longer nauseous," she muttered to herself as she approached her house.

She felt relieved of the stress and all that tension that had been bottled up inside her. She closed the door behind her. She thought of what her father had said, and wondered why he called her friend a 'Wop,' but hummed a tune instead. With stealing the pen, she also felt the anger at her parents slowly dissipate.

Rosalina had no idea that her good friend was jealous about Bart when she called her on the weekend. "Come on over, Justine. We can listen to some music and watch some videos," she said. She then added in a whisper, "My parents will be away, and I invited Bart and his friend Pietro, also. Should be fun, just the four of us, and I have some good marijuana."

Justine didn't think much of Pietro. "Too dull and bookish, a know-it-all," she said to her friend on the phone as she looked at herself in the mirror that late Saturday afternoon. "And he's not interested in me the way Bart is," she added after she hung up. In seething anger, she threw her mobile on the bed. However, she had agreed to be there with some wine.

As she left for the party that weekend, her father shouted down from the top of the stairs, "Remember: home by midnight." And her mother added as Justine was out the door, "And no drugs, Justine; you'll be grounded if I smell that dope on you again."

As Justine slowly walked the next block to see Rosalina, she was uptight, tense, and worried about her parent's threats. And she felt worse than she had on Monday, with her breathing coming in short spasms and her chest in pain. She was apprehensive as to what she would find with Bart's behavior that evening.

As she walked into Rosalina's house she was only interested in Bart and what might happen with Rosalina with the light low and the music on. She was thinking of some way to get Pietro on that couch with her friend and Bart all to herself.

As she was welcomed by Rosalina and poured herself a glass of wine, she could feel her heart racing again. It was all about her father's threat and watching Bart talking to Rosalina. Her chest was about to explode from the tension.

The night didn't happen as she had hoped. As the evening progressed, she was furious to see Rosalina coming onto Bart. Even worse, he was responding to her seductive advances. As she sat alone across from the two lovers, Justine watched Pietro. He was by himself on a chair and only interested in talking about Shakespeare, Byron, and other poets.

Justine, alone on another chair, puffed on her joint, swilled down gulps from the white wine she'd brought and quietly fumed. She tried desperately to control her anguish. She watched Rosalina's hands moving along Bart's thighs on the sofa in the dim lights.

In order to interrupt Bart from continuing to caress Rosalina, she came up with the bright idea to embarrass her friend in front of Bart. "Listen up, guys. I know that some people refer to your family as 'Wops,' so where the hell did such a derogatory term come from?" she asked pointing to Rosalina as she finished her third glass of wine.

Rosalina brushed off the question and continued caressing Bart. However, it was bright-eyed Pietro who got up from where he sat across from Justine and started to expound in a very scholastic and academic manner.

"Why are they, the Italians, called that? Well, I'll tell you all about it. I studied that in the American history course that I took last year."

Rosalina was about to tell him to sit down, shut up and have another toke, but Bart hushed her up, as he was busy unbuttoning her blouse.

Pietro continued, in a very professorial way. "With Out Papers. W.O.P. It was when they, the Italians and all those like, ahem, ah, Rosalina's distant family, came through immigration at Ellis Island in New York. At the turn of the century."

Rosalina looked embarrassed but, to Justine's nervous jealousy, she watched as Bart consoled Rosalina with his one arm tight around her shoulders and his other hand up her blouse. "For Christ's sake, man, just sit down and have a drink," Bart said, fondling Rosalina's breast.

Pietro ignored that and just continued. He was on stage and pompously added, "They, the poor Italians, had no proper visa papers, documents, or passports. The immigration officers looked askance at the destitute families and just stamped 'W.O.P.' across their immigration forms, 'without papers.' That was it: calling out, 'here's another wop,' to the medicos behind them, to examine them for tuberculosis or any other communicable illnesses."

The lecture ended, Pietro looked about, smiled, and waited for a thundering, rousing ovation. He didn't get it and so he did sit down and poured himself some wine. This just made Justine more furious to see Bart caressing her friend and Pietro showing off.

Justine pushed herself off the edge of the chair and ignored Pietro, who was now coming close to her. He had some of his own ideas, since the lights were low and the wine flowing.

Justine got up and staggered to her friend. "Rosie, I need to pee," she whispered, knowing that her friend hated being called by that name. Justine grimaced to see Bart remove his hand from inside her friend's skirt.

Rosalina pushed her skirt back down over her knees and looked up at Justine. "Upstairs, sweetie. Second door on the right," she answered and lit another joint for Bart.

She and Bart waited until Justine was up the stairs. Bart waved at Pietro to have another drink from the bottle of wine and returned to what he and Rosalina were happily doing best.

Justine stopped at the top of the stairs, looked down at Bart, and gave him the finger. As she walked down the hallway, she ignored the second door on the right and walked into Rosalina's bedroom. She had been there often when visiting her now not-so-good friend.

A small table lamp, switched on low beam, was on at the bedside. Justine's heart was racing, and she felt like throwing up, but she was just able to suppress that feeling in her guts. She swore to herself and knew that her nausea was all Rosalina's fault.

At that moment, her eyes fell on all of her friend's jewelry on the dresser table. She turned the lamp on high. "Ah, nice earrings," she said as she picked up the two pearl earrings and quickly put them in her slacks pocket.

She then opened the top drawer in the dresser table. It was full of Rosalina's underwear, bras, panties, silk pajamas, and dozens of pairs of stockings. "She won't miss these. Pretty pink," she said quietly to herself as she stuffed the pink silk panties into her purse.

Justine turned the lamp back on low beam and quickly left that room. She went into the bathroom, flicking on the light and locking the door. She was surprised that her stomach had stopped heaving and her nausea had cleared.

She took the earrings out of her pocket and tried on one pearl earring. "Nice, pretty pearls. I'll wear them next weekend at the mall. Rosie will be out of town at the lake with her parents. Won't miss them," she said as she admired herself in the mirror. Her chest was calmer, and the spasms had softened.

She stripped down, took the panties out of her purse, and tried them on. She stood up. Suddenly, her heart had stopped racing and was back at a calm, normal rate, and her chest pain had cleared. She took her pulse. Quiet, even, and slow. She felt the tension fade away.

She turned and flushed the toilet, stripped off the stolen panties and put them back in her purse, dressed, and walked out.

"I'll wear them too, when I go to the mall shopping," she mumbled to herself as she walked down the stairs.

"What time is it?" Pietro asked as he pointed at Justine and put a joint into the ashtray. Justine looked at Bart but didn't make eye contact with Rosalina, who was tucking her blouse back into her skirt.

"One o'clock. Oh, shit. I better get home," Justine cried out as she walked to the front door.

"See you when I get back from the lake, dearie," Rosalina shouted out. Justine gave a wave and left.

Justine walked on the double down the street and was relieved to get home just half an hour before her parents walked in. She went to her room, secreted the earrings and the silk panties under her mattress, turned her bed lamp off, and crawled into bed.

She ignored Rosalina at school that week and stayed out of Bart's sight. But all that week she again felt shaky, nervous, and tense. She had already vomited twice at home and again in the school bathroom. Her teacher had told her that she was on the verge of failing her English class.

"Shit, I should have listened to Pietro," she cried in bed that night.

That weekend she was more anxious, and her heart was racing again, fluttering, and skipping beats. "I know it was because of that creep, Bart," she yelled at herself in the mirror. She prayed that going to shop at the mall would quiet her rage down.

She was scratching at her face, nervous and needing to vomit again as she walked into the large department store. Justine took the elevator to the ladies section, but felt like heaving up her lunch. She was worried about getting diarrhea again.

She felt her pulse racing. She was still overwhelmed by her mother's accusations. "I was changing your bed sheets, Justine, and discovered these earrings and someone else's underwear. You need help, dear. Maybe our doctor can refer you again for therapy for your kleptomania, dear."

She knew that it was that threat from her mother, plus failing her English test, that had gotten her so nervous. And then loosing Bart to Rosalina, which made her depressed and even more angry.

She too didn't need her mother's lecture that morning, similar to Pietro expounding on history. "Klepto, as I recall, is derived from Greek, meaning to steal. Mania means a neurotic condition: madness, dear. That, I fear, is what you might have," her mother said as she put the panties and earrings on the table in her room. She left her mother and the house in a huff to get to the mall.

Once in the mall, she was ready to vomit. "Thank God the ladies room was on this floor," she said to herself as she ran into the ladies room, locked the door, knelt over the toilet bowl, and heaved up her breakfast. She heaved a few times and then sat down and took in several deep breaths to relieve the tight stress in her chest. It was all related to her mother's scolding and the embarrassment of her finding the panties and earrings.

Justine felt better as she returned to the young women's clothing department. She walked about and admired three very expensive sweaters on the rack. The clerks were busy folding sweaters as Justine asked, "Can I try these three on to see how they fit?"

The elderly clerk pointed to the small fitting rooms in the corner. "Yes, over there, miss."

Justine nodded and took all three into the small room, closed the door, and removed her long summer overcoat. She tried all three on, one at a time. "Beautiful. I'll take it," she said to herself in the full-length mirror as she put her coat on over the one sweater that she liked.

As she handed two of the sweaters back she smiled. "Thanks, Margaret," she said as she read the clerk's name tag. "Don't fit me too well, and the color doesn't suit me." She walked away.

Justine slowly and nonchalantly walked past the perfume counter farther down the aisle, smelling this and that on the counter. She took her time, smiled at the older woman behind the counter, and used the counter spray of perfume on her wrist.

An older lady was fussing over which body powder to buy, and the clerk was busy showing her various samples. As the clerk knelt down to retrieve a box, Justine slid a small Dior perfume bottle up her sleeve and slowly walked away.

At the entrance door to the mall, she was surprised by how well she felt. Her gut had settled down, the pain in her chest was gone, her breathing was calm, and her heart was no longer skipping a beat. Her gut was quiet again.

At the entrance door she was surprised to see a police car at the curb with lights flashing. Justine turned to find a man, a security officer, at her side. She reared back as he tapped her on the shoulder.

"Sorry to frighten you, miss, but can you show me that beautiful sweater under you coat?" he asked kindly as he held her arm.

Justine balked and wanted to push the man in the striped yellow jacket away. "No, I … well … I paid for it," she answered with a quiver in her voice. She tried to leave, but he held on with a strong grip.

"Also, that bottle of perfume that I saw you put up your sleeve and into your purse just now, miss. Can you show me the receipts?" he asked as he held her arm and waved to the policeman in the cruiser.

Justine's stomach rumbled. She thought she would have to throw up right there and then. She swallowed hard and tried to compose herself. She answered with a quiver in her voice, "A receipt … well … ah … I threw them away. Um … didn't need them anymore."

The security man was very calm and courteous. "We … that is, Margaret and I, have you on camera, miss. I watched you at the perfume counter also. You're either a professional thief or you suffer from kleptomania, miss."

"Klepto-what? What is that?" she asked as she was escorted out to the police cruiser, knowing the answer. She knew she was now in trouble.

At the door to the cruiser, the security man said politely, "I'll have to call your parents, miss. They will help you at the police station."

"Parents? No, no. Don't call my father, please. Ask for my mother, please. She will talk to you. My mother only, please," she pleaded, as she cried into a tissue.

The security officer turned away and dialed the number that Justine gave him. He told the policeman holding the door open for Justine to look after her and wait as he phoned.

He returned to face Justine after the phone call. "Your mother: I did ask for her as you wished," he said as a number of shoppers stopped to see what was going on.

"Thank God. What did she say? What did she say?" Justine asked again, blubbering into her tissue over her mouth.

"She said that she would see you at the station and get you home after the clerk signs the arrest warrant. Said to tell you that she loves you in spite of your disorder, and not to worry."

The policeman ushered Justine into the open car door. "She did? She said that? That she loved me in spite of what I did.

My disorder, she called it?" Justine asked, relieved as she slid into the backseat of the cruiser.

"Yes. That's what your mother said to me," the security man replied as he closed the back door. He added through her open window, "Your kleptomaniac disorder, miss. She also called it such. She added that she'll take you for therapy real soon."

He watched the cruiser car slowly make its way through the heavy mall traffic as the several onlookers walked by. One older man in the crowd pointed his finger at the security guard and sneered, "Damned thieves. They the type that make our prices go sky-high in these here shops. Should lock them all up and throw the keys away."

KLEPTOMANIA

As Justine's mother explained to her daughter in the above fictionalized story, the word "kleptomania" is derived from Greek, and means "to steal."

The criteria for the diagnosis is considered by medical and psychiatric authorities to include a recurrent failure to resist the impulse to steal objects that are not usually required for personal use or financial gain. This also includes the added feeling of increased tension or other emotion at some point prior to the theft. Also, at the time of the theft or very soon after, there is a feeling of pleasure, gratification, and a complete relief of the uncomfortable emotion experienced prior to the theft.

Likewise, the diagnosis must include a total inability to defend against the urge to steal, and the disorder must not be due to some other, more obvious, mental illness. However, the incontrollable stealing can lead to an additional debilitating mental disorder, such as obsessive-compulsive disorder, depression, or severe physical anxiety, as Justine demonstrated with her vomiting and cardiac stress.

Both the initial kleptomania and the added disorders then complicate and impede a normal, productive life. The diagnosis can produce much shame and guilt and usually involves additional serious legal problems, as it did with Justine. It could then have a great effect on the sufferer's relationships, education, employment, and family.

As to the financial and economic aspects, kleptomania is now more common than previously thought. This is due to the advent of technology used by businesses with computerization, cameras, and plain-clothes security people. It is now considered to account for a very large percentage of shoplifting costs and a major loss to the business economy.

The statistics indicate that it is considered to begin in late adolescence or early adulthood. It is more prevalent in women by a ratio of 3:1 for females. Furthermore, there is the component of an obsessive-compulsive aspect to the personality. That is, the individual becomes obsessed in their perfectionistic thinking to continue being preoccupied with how and what to steal.

Finally, if drug and alcohol addiction becomes a problem in an attempt to reduce the symptoms, then this becomes an added complicating factor of encouraging the disorder.

The kleptomaniac already suffers from anxiety or depression, both prior to or soon after stealing. That person can then later on suffer other, more severe emotional effects with this disorder, which includes guilt, shame, more severe chronic depression, or severe chronic anxiety.

Also, there can be other disturbing, intrusive obsessive thoughts that become disabling with excessive stress, insomnia, remorse, and added despair. Friends and families are severely affected, incarceration is frequent, and employment can be terminated.

The multiple "minor" emotions have already been listed, but in kleptomania there may be more major mental disorders that are concurrent, coexisting, or co-morbid. Multiple can occur at once; examples include severe overwhelming anxiety disorder, eating disorders, bipolar disorders, and other, more serious depressive disorders or substance abuse.

Together with the above major concerns are the potential severe substance abuse issues and conduct disorders like antisocial personality disorder. Another major concern, with the production of so much guilt and shame due to familial and legal consequences, is the attempts at suicide, which could be accidentally or intentionally fatal.

There are a number of very famous Hollywood starlets who have been arrested for this unfortunate disorder. Some have been discovered stealing from jewelry shops and well-known stores that sell expensive clothing apparel. They have been charged, arrested, and fined, and some cases placed on probation.

Treatment of kleptomania can be difficult since the individual is so secretive, and their partners or families may not come forward due to shame. Often, the person enters therapy only after multiple detections and apprehensions that include legal consequences and incarceration.

Nevertheless, treatment can have an excellent outcome, that is, prognosis, if the person is willing and compliant to therapy. A referral to a qualified psychologist is essential; cognitive therapy with that therapist is most beneficial. Group therapy is very helpful, and this may include the family in group therapy, family therapy, or just with the individual.

The family physician may have the time and the education to be a therapist, but a referral to a psychiatrist may be most productive, both for individual psychotherapy and for the addition of medication. There is now excellent medication for the obsessive and compulsive aspect of the disorder, or for the other underlying mental problems.

Medication may also be required for any of the more serious aspects of the disorder, as explained above. Finally, the person's spiritual or religious mentors may also be most therapeutic in harmony with the other therapies.

ARNOLD, THE PEDOPHILE

Everyone loved Arnold, as he was a very sociable, pleasant man, and Arnold loved everyone. Especially young boys. He was in his early fifties, tall, dark, handsome, and in great physical shape: he jogged daily, went to the gym often, and only ate a healthy diet. All his lawyer friends and the paralegal staff in the law firm where he worked admired him for his tenacity, reliability, good friendship, and legal expertise.

The minister of music at his local Baptist church in Ottawa was thrilled that he had established a boys and girls mixed youth choir. They sang regularly at the Sunday services, and the congregation and head minister were overjoyed with the large attendance.

The Boy Scouts of Canada were also pleased to have him form a large group of dedicated young Cubs in the Ottawa community. They made him the Akela, their leader.

Arnold often invited some of the youth in his Cub group to his home to teach them how to prepare for camp outings in the coming springtime. He would lecture to the boys and to the parents, some of whom assisted him. "The ice in the lakes will be gone soon, and the weather is warming. We have to follow the Scout motto, gentlemen: 'Be prepared.'"

The boys and those fathers who assisted Arnold agreed to the extra weekend, since he provided appetizers and lots of cola drinks for the youth and beer for the fathers.

"Since we don't have enough time during our regular evening meetings, then those who can will learn at my home on some weekend day. That is, how to make proper knots with ropes, how to make a safe fire in the woods, and how to set up a tent," he proudly instructed the group.

He invited some of the fathers to participate in those meetings. He again added proudly, "As the fatherly presence will solidify the bonding amongst the group."

As time wore on, those few fathers who attended at his home left earlier on those weekends to be with their wives. "I'll make sure your boys get home safely," he assured those fathers. As spring arrived he was admired by the community, the Cubs, and their parents for taking the group camping every summer.

Until a father of one of the boys registered a complaint.

Mr. Albertson, one of the fathers who always had to leave early without his son, wrote a letter to the provincial Scout leader. His son had been tearful as he described the abuse to his father. Albertson complained that Arnold had been touching his young son inappropriately one evening at his home while learning to tie knots, and then on another occasion at the summer camp while his son was in his sleeping bag.

Although everyone agreed that it didn't sound like Arnold at all, and Arnold calmly asserted that it wasn't true, that following week he was called to have a personal meeting with the provincial Scout Master in downtown Ottawa.

"Mister McArthur, you are now aware of the copy of this father's letter, plus that which I wrote to you personally," he said in a very courteous manner while Arnold was standing before the Scout master's desk in his Ottawa office.

Arnold didn't flinch and only nodded as the Scout master reread the embarrassing letter which detailed the gross misdemeanor with the father's young son.

"I also had a phone meeting with your Scout leader in Halifax when you were a Cub leader there. Although you left them suddenly when you moved here to Ontario, they have no record of issues with you. However, the Boy Scouts of Canada will receive a copy of this complaint and my letter to you, and you will be discharged from your post as a Cub leader."

Arnold didn't put up a fuss and left with no charges having been laid, since the boy's story couldn't be verified. But Arnold and his mother did have to go through a number of embarrassing interviews with the RCMP. Arnold had gone through this before, as he shamefully recalled.

"Not only in Halifax, Arnold. But also in New Brunswick, where you again had to move for similar reasons," his mother reminded him as she comforted him with a hug at dinnertime.

He still felt remorse and shame for his actions back then and for embarrassing his mother, who always moved with him. He had always regretted having to leave his mother alone so he could attend his studies after his father had moved out during Arnold's late teens. At that time, his mother had agreed to the separation since his father drank heavily and often admonished Arnold, "For not being a real man."

However, he was fortunate to get a position with the law firm in New Brunswick and then again when he moved to Ottawa.

As the provincial Scout leader was explaining his decision, Arnold was thinking of telling him of a possible solution. That he would assure him that he would enter therapy again for his personality disorder. He finally decided that he shouldn't do that, as he wanted to keep his past pedophilic history to himself.

For the time being.

After receiving the Scout director's complaint, it was his mother who sat him down after the dinner meal at home the day before he moved out west. "Arnold, baby, I know that you have also lost your youth choir after the church minister spoke to you about you-know-what. That church minister, Reverend Follows, did the same in suggesting therapy."

"I remember him. Nice guy, but I … um … don't need that kind of therapy."

"It was what that psychiatrist offered you, or you'll have to move again someday, darling boy. For your partiality for young boys," she said sadly as she offered him dessert.

Arnold sat quietly but grew increasingly anxious. He sipped on his third glass of wine after dinner to calm his nerves. Finally, he looked up at his elderly mother, stuttering, "Remember, Ma? I asked you … um … not to refer to me as your baby, or darling boy, Ma. Remember? Doctor Smithers? I can't go through that … ah … kind of therapy, Ma."

"He said that it would cure you, Arnold," she said kindly as she cleaned the dishes off the table.

"Yeah, but … er … ah … ten electroshock treatments to rewire my brain, or LSD therapy for months on end in a clinic? Or female estrogen hormones for life?"

His mother came over to him and lovingly brushed his wisp of graying hair back over his ears. "Well, maybe that's too drastic.

But the hormones might help on a long-term basis."

Arnold almost gagged on his glass of wine. "Those are female hormones. Like, progesterone or … ah … something like, ah, estrogens. I'll lose all my nice hair and probably grow breasts. My God almighty, Ma, you don't want … ah, to see that on me," he pleaded, becoming more anxious with the hemming and hawing as he spoke.

His mother noticed him getting more anxious and drinking more, like his father had. She was quiet for the longest time. "If you move to Vancouver, like you said last night, then you might meet up with your father," she suggested sadly, but added hopefully, "Or perhaps meet a nice young lady."

Arnold had always been very empathetic to his mother's emotions from an early age. "Sad, um … are you, Ma? How come? I never … um, knew why Father moved out to go so far away."

He waited as his mother became contemplative. "He told me that he found someone much younger who would listen to him. He complained that you and your twin brother were more important than he ever could be in the home: that I had no time for him. Never listened to the stress he had as the owner and manager of his law firm in town. That whiskey calmed him down, I guess."

"I remember that he often said that I was the, ah, apple of your eye, Ma. And my brother, Alwyn, also."

"Yes, that was why your father moved from Wales years ago. His parents always fought and complained that Alwyn, their grandson, was always living with other young men. Your pa never returned to Wales, and that was why you and I came to Canada: to get away from his parents."

His mother wiped a tear away. She turned to finish washing the few dishes from dinner. "Maybe you'll meet up with him in

Vancouver. Maybe he'll give you a position in his law firm. Maybe … he's still with that … younger woman," she said as she blew her nose in her apron.

That next day Arnold packed his belongings. He also gathered up the many illicit magazines that he had secreted from years ago of young children and tore them up, destroying them in the garbage can. However, he still liked his videos of young children, especially the videos of boys, which he had bought in the porn shop. He packed them in his suitcase, well-hidden under all his clothes.

That morning Arnold kissed his mother goodbye, nervous and sweating, but reassured her, "Father continues to send you the … ah, the alimony, Ma. He's … ah … a good man and set up a trust fund for you. I'll keep in touch with e-mails and we can always talk, you know … er, over the phone."

He drove his old Toyota Tercel to BC, stopping periodically to rest in a motel and watch his videos on the motel TV. Once he established himself in central Vancouver in an old rooming house and secreted his porn videos in a closet, he called his father. He was thrilled with his father's response in wanting to see him, and they had lunch together two weeks later.

As he sat across from his father in the restaurant, he was surprised to realize that his father was now in his early seventies.

"You're a fine-looking young man, Arnold. Always was and still are. I was sorry to hear about the church and the Scouts. Thanks for being so straightforward with what happened; sure, you'll be welcome to the firm. McArthur, Petroff, and Willis Law firm can use a smart, young lawyer, like yourself."

Arnold munched on his Caesar salad. He had stopped drinking and just sipped on his Perrier water. "The psychiatrist told me to … ah, stop drinking, as it reduced my cognitive will, which is why I refused when you suggested the … um … wine for lunch. He said it weakened my resolve as to my … er, personality problem, Father."

They never talked further about his pedophilic tendencies, but it was well understood by his father. "I hear as we talk that you still have that stammer, Arnold. You always had that from childhood when anxious," his father said as they walked out into the Vancouver downpour.

Arnold felt embarrassed but explained, "Yep, my therapist … um … said it was due to my closeness to my ma and some genetic stuff, like with my twin Alwyn. We talked a lot about my … um … relationship to her. But she, ah, was a good mother to me."

"Yes she was, and always will be, son. She always said that she accepted you as you are, even with that disorder, and would always love you," his father said. He gave Arnold a hug as they parted.

That next week, Arnold was indeed accepted by the others in his father's busy law firm in downtown Vancouver. It was a few months later that he became very friendly with Angelina, one of the older, Asian-American paralegal secretaries who was very kind and helpful to him.

"She reminds me of mother. Very kindly and supportive," he once said to his father in his office as they discussed how to handle an automobile accident case.

His father was pleased with the work Arnold was doing and told him so when he called him into his office some few weeks later. They chatted about his excellent work ethic, but then his father commented as Arnold was leaving, "Angelina is a nice lady, son. She would be good for you, and you would be good for her, Arnold. She and her family are heavily invested in land, herbal medicine, and apartment buildings locally," he said with a sly wink.

It wasn't long after that conversation that he married Angelina.

He was good for her, and he accepted her scoliosis, her limp, and her need for a cane as she walked. She accepted his past history, which he slowly confided in her before they married, and she was kind to him in helping him with his despair of leaving the east and trying to deal with his pedophilic problem.

He had destroyed his videos, as she suggested.

Arnold's father met him in the firm's coffee lounge soon after the wedding. "After all, son, I agree that marriage looks good on you."

Arnold nodded and finished his latte. "She's insisted on treating my predilection … um, ah … for you know what, with all kinds of herbal medication from her uncle's alternative medicine pharmacy," he answered with some embarrassment. He added, "It works, but I … ah … no longer have any desire for her … ah, but Angelina said it's okay, since she doesn't like to be bothered that way anyhow."

His father smiled and thanked him for being so honest. He comforted Arnold with his arm around his shoulder. "Angelina's a nice lady, and the Oriental community that you now live in is happy with the marriage. And also the firm is very pleased, I hear," his father said.

His father gave him a big hug again, told him that he loved him, and added, "My new wife, not that girl I left with, would like the two of you to come and have dinner at our place this weekend."

"That's great, Dad; thank you, and thank her very much," Arnold answered, working hard not to stammer.

Arnold was pleased to have met his father's new wife. All four had a grand evening, but Arnold wondered if Katharine, his father's wife, knew all about his past pedophilic history. His desires had been markedly suppressed with the herbal meds, to the extent that he was somewhat indifferent and apathetic. He had read about those side effects online.

Angelina commented on those same side effects when they got home as she removed her back brace to get into bed. She moved in close to him and said, "Dear husband, I see that you still avoided any close eye contact with Katharine. I'll tell you, one of my eldest married uncles, still in China, had a prefrontal lobotomy to cure his love for prepubescent girls. He kept a harem of such girls in another house that he owned and made money on them with all his older men friends."

Arnold reared back and moved slightly away from his wife. Such an open suggestion of a lobotomy cooled any ardor he had for Angelina that night.

Once he recovered he admitted, "One of my earlier psychiatrists told me that he could recommend that treatment, um … but after that I never saw him again. Where, ah … did that treatment ever come from?"

Angelina was pleased to feel that his ardor had cooled. She occasionally fulfilled his needs, but only as a duty to her husband. She slowly explained what her uncle had gone through in Shanghai many years ago. "He was arrested for selling young girls that he'd bought from indigent families in the country to other wealthy men in the city. The police locked him up in a prison sanatorium and he was lobotomized."

Arnold sat up and turned on the bedside lamp. "I need some … er … some light. This is so weird, almost scary. So, what happened?"

Angelina held his hand tightly to calm him down. "He was cured of his desires, but was like a zombie afterward; that was when I saw him as a young girl in my teens. I read about that surgery. It was developed by a neurosurgeon, Doctor Moniz, in Europe in 1935. It had been observed for centuries that people who were strange, odd, or insane were cured after the front of their heads were badly injured in an accident or during a war.”

“Moniz? Sounds like that psychiatrist of mine, Doctor Mauthausen. So, er … what happened?”

“Moniz cut the front lobes of animals, especially aggressive monkeys, and found them to be cured of their aggression. Over 20,000 lobotomies were performed in the United States by the early 1950s.”

“My God. And in, ah, your China? What happened to Moniz?”

“Yes, but they don’t publish such statistics. There have been over 30,000 across Europe. Moniz was awarded the distinguished Nobel Prize just before the war broke out in the ‘40s. Heavy tranquillizers were developed in the late 1950s that essentially had the same effect. LSD was also commonly prescribed as a therapy in the ‘70s for personality disorders.”

“Glad I wasn’t arrested and had my brains cut,” he said, holding onto Angelina. He turned the light off and pulled the covers over her.

Angelina had one more bit of information as she snuggled up to him. “Yes, dear. It was Stalin, in Russia, who outlawed the use of prefrontal lobotomy. Said it was too drastic a treatment.”

“Good for Uncle Joe.”

“Don’t forget, dear husband. Take the herbals in the morning. Drink them with your tea,” his wife said. She kissed him good night and then pulled the covers tight over Arnold.

PEDOPHILIC DISORDER

Pedophilia (also spelled paedophilia) is a psychiatric disorder in which an adult or older adolescent experiences a primary or exclusive sexual attraction to prepubescent children. It is termed a disorder in the Diagnostic Manual of Mental Disorders and is a sustained pattern of sexual arousal as manifested by persistent sexual thoughts, fantasies, urges, or behaviors involving prepubescent children.

It was first formally recognized as a character disorder in the late 19th century, and at first was documented to only occur in men. It was later found that it also occurred in women. The diagnostic criteria include:

1. Over a period of at least 6 months there are recurrent, intense, sexually-arousing fantasies, urges, or behaviors involving sexual activity with a prepubescent child or children (generally age 13 years or younger).

2. The individual has acted on these sexual urges or fantasies, which cause marked distress or interpersonal difficulty.
3. The individual is at least 16 years of age and at least 5 years older than the child.

There are those pedophiles who are only sexually attracted to males, and then there are those who are only attracted to females. Some pedophiles are attracted to both sexes. A useful diagnostic indicator to determine their specific needs is the need for pornographic material depicting prepubescent children, whether male, female, or both sexes.

The incidence is generally uncertain, but some authorities place it at 3-5% in men and possibly a fraction less for women.

Other types of personality disorders may have a predilection for pedophilia, by intent or accidental, and may only be sporadic. This could include antisocial personality disorder, obsessive-compulsive disorder, early cognitive disorder (as in Alzheimer's or traumatic brain disorder), and the substance and alcohol abuse type of personality.

The basic cause of pedophilia is not yet known. Some testing of such criminals has discovered a potential link between the disorder and a lower IQ, with poor scores on memory testing, scholastic failure, and earlier head trauma with loss of consciousness. A genetic factor is still uncertain, as is a lower testosterone level in male pedophiles.

Most pedophiles are male and most prefer the opposite sex. However, it is considered that if the male is basically immature and has difficulty forming a close bond with mature males, then his choice could be male children. Similarly, if the male is basically heterosexual but very immature in nature and unable to form a close relationship with adult females, then his choice may be young girls.

In many cases the adult pedophile is known to the affected, abused child. Such an adult may be a family member or a person of authority (teacher, instructor, or coach). Some pedophiles are attracted only to those children who are related to them, and can thus be more easily available and are easier targets. Thus the pedophilic activity becomes one of incest.

Treatment of pedophiles is very difficult. Prior to the advent of psychiatric therapy, the pedophile who was incarcerated in a mental hospital or in a prison could be subjected to a variety of treatments. Such treatments offered or imposed could be castration (removal of the testicles) or prefrontal lobotomy (surgical cutting of the frontal lobes).

Multiple electroshock therapies to "rewire" the brain was also not uncommon. Heavy sedation with multiple tranquillizers or the use of lengthy LSD regiments was also a treatment, but long-term observation was essential and very difficult. The use of female hormones for men or male hormones for women was also a form of therapy.

None of those above stated attempted treatments was ever successful. They often caused serious mental or physical side effects that were disabling, which in turn may have discouraged further pedophilic activity.

Present-day treatment remains difficult because of noncompliance, unless the person is under the direction of a spouse, other family member, or a probation officer throughout the lengthy procedure. However, if the person is interested, willing, and compliant, then treatment of this character disorder can be very favorable.

The family doctor may be the first to offer therapy, or a referral to a qualified psychologist may be necessary. Long-term individual cognitive therapy and/or group therapy is most helpful. The spouse or other family member should be involved.

A referral to a psychiatrist may be essential in order to evaluate other personality disorders or early dementia. Tranquillizers or hormone therapy may be required, with the assistance of the appropriate hormone specialist.

The prognosis can be very optimistic, depending on acceptance and total compliance on a long-term basis. Such treatment together with family members, or partners who are willing and able to be involved, can be most helpful.

CARMELITA AND HER PIMP

He found her half-awake, half-asleep, resting on a bench in a small Vancouver park in the downtown east side. It was early morning in late July when he nudged her legs aside to make room for himself. He smiled as he sat down at the far end, silent. Roberto patiently waited until she stirred fully awake and watched as she held her small suitcase tight against her body on the bench.

"You're awake, little one? Did your boyfriend kick you out? What's your name, little one? Nowhere else to sleep? Are you working today? I might have a job for you," Roberto lied as he lit up a joint and gently tickled her ribs as she rubbed her eyes and sat up next to him.

He preferred younger girls in their early teens, but this one would do, he thought as she looked up at him. She had good teeth when she smiled, long, flowing fair hair, and clear but darker skin. Her fingernails were dirty, but she had a decent figure, with nice legs under her skirt and full breasts under her sweater. But she needed a good scrub. In his bathtub. He would help her.

He would gladly do that for her, he thought, as he ran his hand along her front and tickled her breasts.

Carmelita giggled with the teasing, sat up more erectly, and rubbed her face to get some flush in her skin. She wasn't sure which of the many questions to answer first.

As the warm sun slowly rose higher she squinted at the man. He looked nice enough: fortyish or older; long, obviously dyed, blondish hair, and a beard that was poorly trimmed. He wore expensive Levi's, smart shoes, and a pricey leather jacket over a clean shirt.

She thought she could trust him, unlike her ex-husband. "No. I don't have work. I was a waitress in Havana ten years ago, and then in Prince Rupert. My husband was from Cuba, and he helped his countrymen escape on his fishing boat to Florida. He drinks, won't work, hit me, and now has a young girl in his bed. He hits me. Often. Carmelita. I'm Carmelita," she repeated and showed the man the bruise on her shoulder.

"Nice to meet you. Me, I'm Roberto. Lived in Cuba once, too. Knew Che, Castro's brother. Long time ago," he lied as he touched the bruise on her shoulder and slid his hand down to her breast, squeezing it gently.

Carmelita didn't wince as she let his hand rest there. She looked impressed as she surveyed him slightly longer and thought he could be kindly to her. Roberto, on the other hand, thought he had a live one.

She was tiny, attractive enough, with a good firmness to her body. She had a decent face, and her English was good enough. "I might have a job for you. I partly own a restaurant close by. On Hastings," he lied again. "Nowhere to live, Carmen, since your no-good husband threw you out? You still have an accent: Cuban?"

"Yes, si. Carmelita. It's Carmelita. My name. Yes, I need to work. My husband didn't give me enough money. And it was me; I left him night before last and took the overnight bus from Prince Rupert. Can I have a toke?" she asked as she protected her small, leather suitcase closer to her body.

Roberto brought out a small bag and rolled her a cigarette. He was pleased that she could most likely be hooked on drugs. He gladly handed it to her. He lit her cigarette and watched her inhale deeply.

"Tried coke, Carmelita? I have some at my apartment. Come. I have a small extra room. Just your own bedroom and a bath. I'll scrub your back, little one, and you can do me at the same time," he said teasingly.

Carmelita giggled at the thought and moved closer into his side. He was in no rush as he put his one arm around her shoulder and slid his other hand up her skirt. Once again, she didn't flinch.

"Not much to do until late evening," he said, and added to entice her further, "I hope the other three girls who work for me will be at the bar. Good money there." He would call them later to make sure.

Roberto waited until she finished her cigarette. He had time to kill, and prayed that the bar would be busy this weekend with lots of men with lots of booze and lots of money. Roberto took the girl's hand and held it gently.

He smiled when she replied, "My own bedroom? You are so kind. I'm a good worker, a good waitress. I had lots of experience in Havana and up the coast here, in your province. We moved here years ago. To fish, but he just pissed his money away, drinking or snorting the white snow up his nose."

"Sorry to hear that, little one," he replied, but not sorry at all. Roberto loved that kind of history in a young woman. He could use her, he thought, and she could be useful in the bar.

She let his hands wander and felt that she could confide in him. She then told him about the emotional abuse she had suffered in her young years, causing her to be very depressed. "Also that my husband was similar, in being abusive, to my older stepbrother years ago," she added and then complained that she was far too dependent on her husband.

"Sorry to hear that, little one." Not that he was. He liked the fact that she was too dependent on men. "You look like a nice girl. Are you over eighteen? We'll get you a nicer dress and some pretty shoes. I own a lady's dress shop. Close by. Come," he again lied with a toothy smile that revealed some bad teeth up front and foul breath.

"Yes, over eighteen: almost thirty, I am. Oh? A new dress and pretty shoes? How kind of you." She giggled again.

Roberto helped her up from the bench. He took her by the hand and they walked a few blocks to a clothing outlet shop. It was for underprivileged women on Pender Street.

Carmelita hesitated to see the junk strewn about and piled high. As he pushed her into the shop, his hand traveled down to her buttocks. "Nice and firm. Come, come, little one. I just own the lady's department. Annie will find you a nice outfit. I'll buy," he said with a smirk as he squeezed her right buttock again.

Carmelita tittered again but walked in and saw Roberto give Annie a sly wink. Annie was rather disheveled for a clerk in a dress shop. She had matted, unruly hair, no makeup, and sloppy, stained slacks with dirty runners. Annie moved her over to a rack, and Carmelita was thrilled with the dress that was picked out for her.

It looked used but clean as she tried it on in the closet, and the shoes were slightly worn, but they fit her well. The polyester jacket was also a good match. Annie put her old skirt, shoes, and blouse in an old paper bag and handed the bag to her.

Once outside, Roberto again asked her about her age. He didn't want trouble with the police again after that sixteen-year-old Aboriginal waif last week.

He smiled when she answered, "Twenty-nine or thirty, Roberto, not sure. My birthday was last week."

Roberto walked her a few blocks away. "Almost thirty is good. Very good, little one," he said as he unlocked the door to his apartment. It was a walk up to the fourth floor of a seedy rooming house on Hastings Street. He opened it and pushed her in.

She had seen some sordid rooms in the squalid areas of Havana city, but not this bad. It smelled of rancid food, marijuana smoke, and stale wine still in open bottles.

Carmelita reared back as she stepped in. "Roberto! A small mouse ran across the room. I saw it, Roberto." Roberto laughed heartily as he came up behind her real tight and squeezed her breasts. "That mouse? She's just leaving now that I'm home," he said as he pushed her into her bedroom.

He poured her a glass of cheap, red wine and told her to drink. "Here, this will calm you down," he offered. Behind her back he dropped a small tablet of Valium into her glass. He slowly maneuvered her onto her bed. "Let's have a small line," he said sweetly, "before we go to the Golden Lion for your waitress job."

Carmelita's bed was a thin, ratty mattress in the corner of a small, windowless room. It had one chair with three legs and two apple boxes piled high as a dresser. As she drank her wine he stripped her down naked and they both snorted a line of coke as he undressed.

Roberto pushed the board with the cocaine toward her for

another snort. She was already drowsy from the sedative he had secreted into her wine, but snorted a line in compliance.

Carmelita wasn't certain of the next few hours, as she was in a partly-comatose state. She was stirred awake a few hours later by Roberto lying next to her, smoking and sipping from his wine bottle.

"Roberto, you had sex with me," she cried out loud as she got up to dress. She shuddered and became more agitated as she realized that he was a pervert and she had been used while sedated and asleep.

It was getting dark in the room as Roberto got up and pulled on his pants. "It was just okay; you were okay. I used a condom, but wanted to make sure you weren't a virgin. I know that Vincent will be there tonight. Nice man, and pays well, but he doesn't like virgins."

Carmelita just accepted the fact and got dressed. She prayed that she would make some good money that night as she crossed herself and gave a silent prayer to her Jesus.

That Friday evening, Carmelita discovered that the Golden Lion was a seedy bar and not a nice restaurant. Roberto told her that her work as a waitress would have to wait until the next day. She accepted that, since she was still inebriated from more wine, cocaine, and another small dosage of Valium in her glass while she put on some makeup in the grungy bathroom.

Carmelita met three nice girls at a small booth in the Golden Lion, where they all sat and greeted several men who entered. It wasn't long before Lucy, and then Miranda, left with a man to go into a small room at the back of the bar.

Soon after a few more spiked drinks, Vincent arrived at ten. He offered to buy Carmelita a drink as he ushered her into the small room.

Roberto waited for over thirty minutes. "How much did Vincent pay you, little one? He was very quick I see," Roberto asked as he walked into the back room of the bar and watched as Carmelita got dressed.

Carmelita was still drowsy from the spiked wine and the two white lines he had given her at the table. "One hundred and fifty dollars, Roberto. I'll need all that to take care of myself, Roberto."

"Absolutely, Carmen. For sure. Just hand it over, and I'll keep it safe for you. I'll return it to you when we go back to your new home."

This time, Carmelita didn't correct him about her name. She just couldn't think straight: the lights were down low and her head was still spinning.

It was near midnight when they both entered his apartment. Roberto pulled out the large wad of dollar bills that she'd given him, unwillingly. "Lucy and Miranda did well. We'll forget about that third girl. She'll have to stay on the streets. You did good, little one."

Carmelita was still inebriated as she watched him put forty dollars on the kitchen table. "Forty? I get half, Roberto. Seventy-five. You said."

Roberto slapped her hand hard. Her four bills went flying to the floor. "Pick them up," he shouted. "I paid ten for your dress, ten for nice pretty heels, ten for the white line you snorted, and five for the wine you drank at the bar. I should charge you for rent," he added crossly.

Throughout that next month, Carmelita absorbed the abuse from Roberto: physical, psychological, and sexual. She was on antibiotics for her venereal disease infection; she was destitute, now addicted to cocaine, and very dependent on Roberto.

Roberto knew she had gonorrhea; he used a condom most of the time with her, but her clients didn't. "I'll get you to see my doctor again. He's close by, on the corner. He'll cure you of whatever you've got," he said, trying to be kind as he felt her body again.

Dr. Brownstone seemed like a nice doctor as he examined her on the table and took a swab of her pelvic discharge while his nurse watched close by. "Yes, you have the clap, dear girl. No doubt, but an antibiotic prescription will cure you quickly. Make sure the men you have sex with wear a condom, miss."

"Clap? Why do you call it that, Doctor?"

Brownstone sat at his desk and wrote out the prescription for an antibiotic and handed to Carmelita as she finished dressing. "That word, 'clap,' came from the French word '*clapier,*' meaning a rabbit hutch. Rabbits were sexually active and promiscuous. Many years ago, a district in Paris, 'Le Clapier' it was called, was full of prostitutes."

"Oh, my goodness, Doctor. I must be more careful."

"Yes, please do so. Men and women who had a discharge like you do were then known to have visited that 'clapier.' Others would say, aha, so you have the 'clap' madam," he explained as he ushered her out.

In the waiting room the doctor hesitated but asked, "Are you despondent? I observe that you are a sad lady, nervous. From the pelvic examination, I saw many scars and old lacerations. Were you abused as a youngster?"

Carmelita balked and did become tearful. She turned aside in shame, but was glad to see no one else was in that room apart from the receptionist. "Yes, Doctor, I am; and yes, I was. By my older stepbrother in Cuba. He was very cruel and demanding of me in my teen years, for a long time. It hurt me … you know … ah, down there," she explained and pointed down to her pelvic area.

"I can refer you to a good counselor if you wish, young lady.

She can help you."

"Thank you, Doctor. Please do. I need help." she said. She accepted the name of the psychologist from the doctor.

Carmelita did follow through with the therapist, who encouraged her to move into a safe house for women when she talked about Roberto's abusive manner.

Her salvation arrived in the form of Beatrise, a Latvian hooker whom she met in the woman's safe house soon after the therapist's suggestion. Beatrise had befriended Carmelita while they had lunch at a café next door to the safe house.

After Beatrise listened to Carmelita's sad, sorry plight she suggested, "Listen, Carmen. Let's call you by that name. Men will find that more alluring in the hotels where I work. I saved up some cash and I know that pimp, Roberto. Asshole. I have a basement suite in a nice part of town. Come stay with me."

That very night, Carmelita escaped from Roberto while he was still asleep. She had made certain that Roberto was drunk from the cheap whiskey, drugged with cocaine and two tablets of Valium that she had secreted some time ago. He had used her twice in her bed before he passed out.

"Hope I gave you my gonorrhea after that, you prick," she whispered in his ear as she wiped herself clean and listened to him snoring deeply. She had already made certain that he hadn't used a condom during sex that night. Prior to that, she made certain to take her birth control pills.

After dressing, she found his pants and cleaned out the pockets of $1200.00 in cash that was rightfully hers. She also took his bank card from his wallet, planning to clean out the account in the morning. She recalled his pin number quietly to herself as she gathered up her clothes to leave.

"Goodbye Mama mouse and little ones," she said softly to the large rodent as it scampered across the floor. Her six little babies followed her as they ran into the hole in the corner. Carmelita took the dish of yesterday's breakfast, still full of corn flakes and banana, and filled it with milk.

She put the dish down on the floor next to the mouse hole and watched as the babies scampered about, feeding. She quietly blew Roberto a kiss, closed the door behind her, and looked forward to meeting with her friend. After she went to the bank.

"Why were you in the safe house, Beatrise?" Carmen asked as she sipped on her coffee the next morning. She was still nervous, because she feared Roberto would be looking for her.

Beatrise felt Carmen's anguish from across the table and gently held her hand. Carmen calmed down as she looked at her kindly friend and waited for the answer.

"I help out with managing that safe house. Help out in the kitchen and counsel the girls who come in: girls like you. I like to give back what the church that runs the safe house gave to me some time ago."

Carmen smiled for the first time and looked up in admiration of Beatrise. "Maybe I can help there one day, Beatrise," she suggested hopefully. "You know that Roberto, he was not only a pervert, but also a pedophile: a pathetic man, a user, and a predator," Carmen said.

Beatrise smiled knowingly. "Yes, and not very nice, either."

Carmen stifled a laugh. She was impressed with her friend's work ethic to help others. She liked Beatrise: an older woman, almost motherly, kindly, and apparently clean of drugs.

"I was also pimped out by that fucker, Roberto. But I've been clean for two years, and I need someone like you to help me at the big hotels. We could do well together with the rich clientele."

Carmen soon learned what 'doing well' meant. She moved in with Beatrise in a better part of town where Roberto wouldn't think of looking. Beatrise showed her how to dress well, how to use makeup, and how to walk and talk seductively. Carmen had enough money for the new wardrobe, and she looked stunning. They sat at the bars in the several of the best hotels in town.

Their clientele were wealthy men: older, separated or divorced, and free of venereal disease. They accepted the condoms that Carmen always carried, paid up-front, and were never abusive.

The bar men and the door men liked the two, clean, higher class girls in their establishments. They were well paid by the girls to protect them and to send men to them. Business was never better for the girls, the door men, and for the hotel, as the rooms were pricey to rent.

One late night after work Carmen asked Beatrise, "My dear friend, I see that you usually prefer the Asian men. You usually pass the white men off to me. I don't object, but why the difference, Beatrise?"

Beatrise laughed as she got ready for bed. "Good for you; you are very observant, Carmen. I hoped that you wouldn't mind. But the Asians pay better, they don't ask for any funny stuff, they wear condoms, are more polite, and they are quick."

Carmen chuckled together with her good friend. "Maybe, someday soon, you can also send them my way, Beatrise."

Carmen reminded herself to tell that good story to her psychologist when she went to see her next week. She would like that one for her records.

PROSTITUTES, PIMPS, AND CHARACTER DISORDERS

A prostitute is a person of any gender who sells sex in exchange for money, drugs, or whatever else is required for a reasonably safe existence. Typically, women are referred to as a "whore" or a "hooker" and men as a "hustler." Both are commonly called "sex trade workers;" this can include phone sex workers, exotic dancers, and those involved in online pornography.

Prostitution has been known for thousands of years, and the earliest recorded was by the Babylonians back in Ancient Mesopotamia. Many Jewish and Christian scriptures mention this activity; some of these writings refer to it as sinful, but it was also recorded as necessary to prevent rape, adultery, incest, or homosexuality.

There is not much specific diagnostic information known regarding the mental health of sex workers or their pimps. They rarely come forward for treatment, but it is generally considered that the prostitute and the pimp both suffer from some degree of mental illness or character disorder.

In the above fiction story, Carmelita did talk about her early abuse, her husband's abusive attitude, and her eventual dependency on Roberto, her pimp. In her case, the psychologist that she saw could have diagnosed her as suffering from a dependent type of personality disorder. Many are schizoid in nature (that is, very unrealistic), indifferent to abuse, are immature, apathetic, and distant in character.

Some therapists regard such characters to be antisocial personality disorders, substance abuse disorders, avoidant or borderline types, or severe adjustment disorders with chronic depression or anxiety that require drugs or alcohol as sedation. Many have some type of sexual dysfunction disorder due to earlier physical, sexual, or psychological abuse, as Carmelita demonstrated.

Pimps who solicit prostitutes, or madams who ply young workers in brothels, are very astute at recognizing such dependent, character-disordered people, since they easily and quickly become very reliant on the pimp for all their needs.

Of course, some cultures and countries do not consider such behavior to be antisocial or illegal in nature. Some countries or states have legalized prostitution. Amsterdam and Nevada are such examples.

Some places (such as Nevada) do require prostitutes to be medically examined for sexually transmitted diseases on a regular basis. Since those prostitutes do attend their local medical facilities regularly, it has been reported that many have a history of early childhood sexual, physical, or psychological abuse, and later, possibly adulthood abuse.

Furthermore, many suffer from post-traumatic stress disorder, drug dependence, and chronic depressive disorders. Many reported ongoing sexual abuse from their close interpersonal relationships with their partners or family members, often requiring protection in a safe house, if available.

The most exclusive, and some of the most famous prostitutes in history, were "courtesans." They were highly-educated, sought after by royalty, were very loyal, and dependable. They were also not only the providers of sexual favors. Being such a courtesan meant that a woman had special privileges in court, was able to discuss politics, and provide support and advice. Since they were so highly respected, they often carried messages and financial capital between states, countries, and kingdoms.

Throughout Europe, America, and elsewhere, street walkers are not uncommon, as are brothels, massage parlors and strip bars where prostitutes work. Escorts, phone sex workers, and newspaper ads for girls are also available. As stated, such prostitutes usually have some type of character disorder and a history of abuse.

Hustlers are usually younger men who provide sexual services. Once more, most are dependent personality disordered characters who may also have a history of abuse, coincidental intelligence disorder, are drug dependent, or are antisocial in character.

Pimps, as Roberto was in the above fiction story, are those who hustle prostitutes and take a large percentage of their money. They may provide a stable income and a secure residence for the prostitute, but also find appropriate clients for the prostitute both on the street or in bars. They also are generally character disorders of the antisocial type, and usually have a history of substance abuse.

Therapy of prostitutes or of pimps is extremely difficult. They are only introduced to treatment through the police or if they require legal assistance through the courts. Occasionally, a family physician will refer such a person to a therapist if they have an overt drug dependence or is depressed, anxious, antisocial, or suffers from a post-traumatic stress disorder.

Some may be involved in therapy if a close relative or friend intervenes, or a safe house counselor makes the referral. If so, then individual psychological therapy, cognitive therapy, or group therapy can be most beneficial.

A referral to a psychiatrist may be indicated to treat the person with the appropriate anti-depressants for their depression, anxiety, or PTSD. Counseling with a spiritual or religious mentor may also be most helpful.

The overall prognosis may be difficult, but favorable if the person is compliant over a long period of time and has the close support of family or friends. A comfortable, safe, and secure home is essential.

CINDY, A VERY DEPENDENT WOMAN

"But, Archibald, my one and only love, you can't just move out and leave me," Cindy cried out dramatically as she reached out for his hand and clasped it tight.

Archibald took her hand away and slowly took a drag from his cigarette. He blew a smoke ring out in Cindy's direction on the couch and used a toothpick on his molars. "So sorry, Cindy. But not so: I'm not your 'only love.' I was only your fourth one, and you had others. You had three others before me, and I remember Thurston telling me that you were too clinging and dependent on him also."

"Oh, but you were the best. Always so good to your Cindy. You never complained that I was too clingy with you," she said, getting off the couch in their living room and putting her finger through the smoke ring.

Archibald looked at his bags, already packed at the door of their small basement unit. "Sad to do it, Cindy girl, but it was too stifling for me. I'll be okay back with my parents for a while. We can see each other from time to time," he said as he flicked the toothpick away.

That was the moment that Cindy began to weep even more hysterically. She hoped that it would work again; it always had before. "I'll kill myself, lover. I'll hang myself in the bedroom where we made love so often," she cried. She watched his reaction out of her left eye.

"Women don't hang themselves. Too long and too painful. I read about that in my psych books."

"Well, then I'll slice my wrists," she said as she went into the kitchen and brought out a butcher knife, still wiping huge tears from her cheeks and brandishing the knife dramatically in the air.

"Neither that, also," Archibald said with a sly smile on his lips. "Too messy for women: blood all over your nice skirt and on the clean floor."

Cindy thought for a minute. "Well then. Pills. That's it: I'll take an overdose if you leave. You'll be sorry."

Archibald got up and put his BC Lions football jacket on, kissed Cindy goodbye, and went to the door. "We don't have any pills here," he said with a twinkle in his eye.

"Aspirin. Aspirin. I'll swallow the whole bottle. Look, you stay, and we can go back into bed. Do it whatever way you like. Have sex all day, just for you. You're evening shift at the restaurant isn't till seven."

Cindy could never wait until he got home at eleven every day. She did nothing except read her *Allure* and *Elle* magazines. Then she would call her girlfriends, Stacy and Bonnie, and depend on them to take her out for a beer for the evening. "I'll call Stacy. She'll understand. She's good to me."

"Aspirin will just make your stomach heave. Remember the last time, when my shift was two hours late? You couldn't wait for me and wanted to 'teach me a lesson' for being late. You just vomited all that shit up." Archibald said as he picked up his bags and walked out to his car.

Cindy watched Archibald close the door behind him. She went to the kitchen and cleaned her face in the kitchen sink, put the knife away, and looked at the aspirin bottle. She would call Akbar, upstairs. "He's very responsible and dependable," she said to herself.

But first, she would call her mother; she was already fretting about being all by herself again.

She quickly dialed her parent's number for where they lived across town. "Oh, Mother. It's you; I'm so glad that you're home. How are you? But before you tell me, please help me with my vacuum cleaner. I can't get it to work, Mother."

Cindy's mother was used to such pleading questions and remarks from the time Cindy was a child. The school psychologist had told her and her husband that Cindy would grow out of such dependency, but she never had.

"Sure, dear. Just plug it into a socket, push the button, and it will start."

"No, no. Maybe you could come over, have tea, and show me how to run it. I need some help, too, with my job application and then some help with that recipe you gave me for chicken soup," Cindy asked, sobbing and almost pleading.

Her mother was calm, but rolling her eyes at Cindy's father, who listened on the other phone. "The button, dear: there's the button on the vacuum you have to push also. I'll come over next week and help you with that soup."

Cindy had more to say and more to ask, especially now that her father was breathing heavily on the other line, but the phone went dead.

Cindy was fussing about after that call, frustrated with the lack of support from mother. She decided to call Akbar, the young man living with his parents upstairs.

"They are a nice, East Indian family. He'll invite me for dinner if I give him what he always wants in my bedroom," she said, looking in the mirror, talking to herself and putting on more lipstick.

She quickly dialed Akbar, the eldest son of the Swaddy family. "Oh good, you're home, handsome. That asshole, Archie, left me. I'm desperate, handsome: afraid to sleep alone with my bad nightmares."

Akbar already knew the next few lines from Cindy and how the conversation would go.

"I'm feeling so lonely and sick to my stomach, Akbar. Would you like to come down for a drink?" she asked, almost in tears for added effect.

Akbar didn't take too much time to answer. "Sure, Cindy. Sure. Are you finished with your period?"

"Yes, three days ago. Oh, I knew that I could depend on you. You're so good to me. I'm so lonely now. I'll get the wine bottle that you like from the fridge, and I have some condoms for you. The extra-large size," she giggled like a little girl into the telephone.

It didn't take Akbar long to shave and tell his parents that he was working the night shift at the other restaurant. Cindy didn't take long after hanging up to spray herself with the perfume that drove Akbar crazy.

She was at the door, breathing heavily in anticipation and expectation as he walked in. "Oh, Akbar. You're so good to me. I need some help with a tough decision at work. Let's just lie down for a while so we can chat," she cooed into his ear as her hand slid down into his jeans.

Cindy made sure that the chat was short and the sexual flirtation very long. She needed him to stay the night.

The next morning, after a further two hours of dalliance, she cooked him several strips of bacon, toast, tea, and three eggs turned over-easy, which he always liked.

"I'm not sure if I should go to work this weekend, Akbar. Would you if you were me?" she asked as she poured him another cup of tea.

Akbar sipped the tea and brought her over to sit on his knee at the kitchen table. "Sure: you need that job at the bookstore, Cindy," he said, caressing her thighs.

"Oh, but honeybun. The owner, Carson, never helps me with putting all those books on the right shelves. I can never decide what and where they all go with that category stuff on the store computer."

"Just ask him for his advice," Akbar said grudgingly as his hand rested higher up her legs.

"The other lady who works there, Cornelia, just ignored me and told me that I'm too needy. Always asking her for her opinion, she said. I do, but only about the high heels I just bought and my new blouse."

Akbar had other ideas for that morning after his breakfast, as Cindy started kissing and fondling him in the chair. "I saw your shoes in the hallway. Nice, beautiful high heels."

"Oh, do you really think so? Do you really like them? Should I keep them? I'll put them on for you. If you stay the night again, then will you help me with my bank statement and the bills I have to pay? Can't decide which to pay first," she said as she led Akbar back to the bedroom.

"Sure, bring them out and I'll sort them out for you," he answered as he picked her up and carried her to the bed.

"You're so strong, honeybun. Do you think I should ask Carson for a raise? I've been there for a month now, but I'm too shy. Will you stay the day to be with me? I'm so afraid to be by myself."

Akbar nodded as he stripped down. "Sure, sure thing. And the night again, if you wish."

Cindy just lay there passively as he took off her clothes. "Oh, just wait a minute, honeybun. After you help me with my banking, can you help with my grocery list? And my car needs an oil change, but I don't know where to take it."

"Sure, sure. I'll drive you to my mechanic on the corner, and I'll tell him what to do after we're finished here," he said as he pulled the sheets over himself.

Cindy knew that Akbar would leave the next morning. When she got up that evening and dressed she put on her high heels and only a sheer blouse. She strutted about, knowing he liked that.

"Do you think that I should just ask Carson on the phone for a raise, or see him in his office? Maybe I should just quit that job. Cornelia is not very nice to me, either."

Following that night, Akbar got dressed in the late morning. He was exhausted with Cindy making so many demands on him. He would drive her to his mechanic and then tell her he had to get home to help his father in painting his bedroom.

Cindy could sense his impending departure. He always made some excuse to leave her.

"I'll call my mother again later, honeybun. She always gives me good advice about my new shoes and that crappy job of mine," she said, handing him the keys so he could drive her the two blocks.

Akbar left her with the mechanic and walked home.

Cindy found George, the mechanic, very helpful with all her questions. She could call on him at any time, he said, and she was certain of that.

As she walked home, she decided that she would call good old

Edward, the elderly man across the street, to come over. He was recently widowed, and she knew that he needed some company. He'd stay with her awhile, or longer.

"He's so wise as a medical doctor, and he can check my rash on my legs. He'll tell me what airplane to take to visit my cousin in Montréal, and how to rent a car there," she thought to herself as she saw Akbar walking ahead of her. If she walked fast enough, she could catch up to Akbar.

She gave a silent prayer that he would be obliging again.

DEPENDENT PERSONALITY DISORDERS

This type of character disorder is one of several others that features a highly-distinctive type of personality. It is akin to the passive-aggressive, avoidant, schizoid, introverted, and obsessive types of personalities.

However, the major characteristic of the dependent type is a pervasive and excessive need to be taken care of, which then leads to submissive and clinging behavior, along with fears of separation. This usually begins in childhood, as we witnessed in Cindy's fictional story above.

As with Cindy, they have difficulty in making everyday decisions, and require an excessive amount of advice and reassurance from others. Such individuals need others to assume responsibility in most major areas in their lives, as Cindy did with her friends and her mother. Finally, there is difficulty in expressing disagreement, and initiating projects on their own. A dependent personality seeks another relationship if one ends.

Some famous people were deemed to be highly-dependent types. Some, for example, suggested that Marilyn Monroe and Princess Diana were dependent personality disordered types. The movie *Single White Female* depicted very well a story of a woman who was very dependent on her roommate.

During any relationship, a dependent person is afraid to be disagreeable for fear of loss of support or approval. They, again like Cindy, fear initiating projects or doing things on their own due to a lack of confidence.

Some go to great lengths to seek nurturance and support from others, to the point of volunteering to be available at any cost, as Cindy was with Akbar.

If one relationship ebbs and ends, then they immediately seek out others in substitution for fear of being alone with the overpowering need for care and support. If forced to be alone, then they are often overwhelmed with panic, stress and anxiety, depression, and suicidal thoughts.

Thus they may then resort to finding other disturbed characters for comfort, or turn to alcohol or drugs to achieve emotional relief.

Unfortunately, if they do not achieve such support and comfort, then they refer to themselves as stupid, careless, and unworthy. At such times they may end up in relationships where they are psychologically, physically, or sexually abused by more aggressive and highly antisocial characters who take advantage of them.

Social relationships thus become limited due to their pathological needs for support and caring. At some point, they then gravitate to other character-disordered people like the borderline, antisocial, avoidant, and histrionic.

The cause and development of this personality disorder is still uncertain. However, it is thought that chronic physical illness or separation anxiety in childhood or early adolescence may be a strong developing factor. Genetic factors may also be a source.

Culture may be important, as some societies encourage women in particular to be more dependent. But young men may also fall into this category in some cultures.

In term of gender-related studies, it is considered that females are more prone to suffer from dependent personality disorders. However, some other studies report the incidence in males to be similar to females.

It is paramount for therapists to distinguish such characters from other mental disorders that demonstrate dependency. Such other mental disorders are the schizophrenic, schizoid personalities, panic disorders, agoraphobias, PTSD, and chronic severe anxiety and depressive disorders.

Similarly, some physical illnesses must be considered also to cause an abnormal degree of dependency. Examples include ongoing cancers, neurological and muscular disorders, and early senile/cognitive conditions like Alzheimer's.

Treatment can once again be very problematic, as such character disorders are usually only introduced to therapy when the parent or spouse insists on it. However, treatment may be available through the family physician or with a religious pastor or similar mentor if they are qualified.

Psychological counseling with a qualified therapist may be very therapeutic on an individual basis or in group therapy. A psychiatrist may be involved for similar therapy, or medication may be necessary if overt emotional symptoms are evident.

The prognosis can be more favorable if the partner or the family is involved. This encourages the individual to continue in treatment on a consistent, frequent basis and for a prolonged period of time.

Finally, it is important for the therapist to rule out the other potential similar behaviors occurring in those other mental illnesses mentioned, especially in the organic, senile, or brain-trauma injuries so common now in our society.

CONRAD, THE NARCISSIST

"You bought another car after only two years, Conrad? What for? That Ford was just fine, sweetheart," Conrad's wife, Tatiana, asked sheepishly as he walked into their palatial house after work. Tatiana stepped back from her second husband, knowing that he didn't take lightly to criticism.

She was right. She recoiled from his rebuke, which was issued with a wave of his hand aimed at her head. "It's what every high-skilled, highly respected professional real estate agent needs these days."

Tatiana nodded respectfully, holding her daughter high for Conrad to lay a kiss on her forehead. "Say hello to Charlotte, Father. She just turned two today," Tatiana said as she dutifully ushered her husband into their living room, which was spotless—just the way Conrad wanted it.

Conrad waved his daughter away. "Don't have time today. Forgot to get her a birthday gift as you wanted: too busy making money for you and this Charlotte baby."

Tatiana was small in stature, blonde, and worked hard to hide her Russian accent, as Conrad insisted. He liked smaller, younger women who admired his height, muscular physique, sharp, chiseled facial features, and trimmed mustache.

Tatiana knew that Conrad was unhappy with having a child; she knew that he needed all of his wife's undivided attention. To soften the expected criticism, she placed Charlotte in her crib in the corner. Tatiana glowed and kissed him on the forehead and bowed ever so slightly to show respect to her husband.

"But Connie, you really did well to buy such an expensive white beauty with silver chrome. You're like my white knight in shining armor with that silver beauty: come to rescue your poor, little Tatiana, and now Charlotte," she extoled.

She knew that he needed such assurance and accolades; otherwise, he had no time for her or for Charlotte. Apart from occasionally in their bedroom, and that was only when he was in the mood.

Conrad took off his new, expensive, tan cashmere coat and hung it on a living room chair. He passed by Charlotte without even a glance. "What the Christ do you know about cars? The best you had was a bicycle until you met me. Jesus almighty, woman, but you were a gorgeous Russian babe when I met you; and you still are pretty for your good man. Apart from your weight since that baby was born," he said, pointing to her belly.

Tatiana sucked in her gut but beamed with the compliment. She took his expensive coat, brushed off some gray hairs, and hung it in the hall closet. "Well that's so, and you have been very good to me in buying us this gorgeous house with outside colonnades. But a big silver BMW SUV? How much did that set us back, Connie?"

Conrad was spitting fire, and his eyes blazed with her questions about money. He was a proud man and always told everyone that he had saved Tatiana from a smelly rooming house that she'd lived in after leaving Russia.

He needed a gorgeous blonde queen on his arm when they went out for dinners. "I need to look good at the office, like I always do. I'll sell more real estate when people see that I can afford this one, babe."

"But Connie …"

"But nothing; and I told you not to call me Connie again. It's Conrad, your beloved knight in shining armor, and I'm the highest-ranking producer in that firm," he again reminded her.

"And so you are, Conn … ah … Conrad. So you are."

"I, and only I, the best husband you've ever had, bring in the most at my office and provide well for you. The staff look up to me for my advice." He snorted as he sat down in the living room, took off his fancy shoes, and told her to bring him some expensive wine from the liquor chest.

Tatiana felt subdued, as usual, but had to continue to work at building up his ego, which always needed constant inflation. "Well, I know so, Conrad. You often tell me that the women in the office love to see you in your new expensive suit, shoes, and ties," she extoled as she picked up Charlotte and gave her a bottle to feed on.

Conrad brought out his iPhone and scanned the photos of himself. "Yes, the pricey shoes. They all admire my pricey shoes and ties, and I know that you are also proud of your husband," he said haughtily. He wiggled his toes, adding, "Come look at my pics standing next to that condo I just sold."

Tatiana came and sat at his feet with Charlotte in her arms. "Beautiful photos. Really, they are. Oh I am very proud of you, really I am. Can we go for a drive to see my father in our new car, Conrad? My father will be impressed when I drive it into his senior's apartment complex. He never saw a car like that in Saint Petersburg."

"Put that kid to bed. I need some quiet time and not a babbling baby in your arms," Conrad shouted.

"Oh, yes, I will, Conrad," Tatiana answered, knowing that he never had time for Charlotte, and probably never would with his important work schedule. "But that car: can I drive it?" she asked again.

Conrad waved her off and grunted again. "Shit, woman, you banged up that crappy old Ford I bought you for a wedding gift. Your seat is always next to your good husband in this car. Not many know how to operate one of these babies. And your poor, senile, demented father was never impressed with me saving you from poverty. But Flo, the chief steno at the office, will go gaga when she sees it."

Tatiana had heard such conceited talk before from Conrad. It was whenever he spoke to Flo on the phone and after he made a big score in real estate. Flo would be so ecstatic. She didn't like the way Flo sucked up to her husband all the time.

Conrad walked into the kitchen, ignoring his wife, who was carrying their child in her arms to put her to bed. "Anyway, I'm busy. Got a big deal to sell that multi-million-dollar complex on the hill," he yelled out to her as he brushed back his fading dark hair in the kitchen mirror.

He stood there, admiring his face, winking, and smiling at the reflection as he plucked a few hairs sticking out of his nose. He took time to lick his finger and smooth out his mustache. He smiled and then took several photos of himself in the mirror, admiring the images.

"Oh, that house will be sold by the best, Conrad. You're the best agent they've ever had. Flo told me that one time when she called for you. Said that you were the only one who could solve her accounting problems and get her books organized," Tatiana said as she followed him into the kitchen with the expensive bottle of red wine.

Conrad puffed himself up and straightened out his tie as he glowed with pride. "She did? She's a smart lady, that Flo. Real smart. Yes, I told her how to balance those books. No one else could do it, she told me."

Tatiana was afraid to tell him that Flo had also told her one evening when she was drunk at the office party that she'd be around if he ever became available. That was when Tatiana had walked away in a huff. She had heard from Jessie, a young Afro-American steno at the office, that Conrad strutted about the office extoling on his virtues.

Jessie had also had too much wine at that office Christmas party last year. Everyone's spouses had been invited, and she and Jessie were talking about clothes in the corner alone. But poor Jessie was fired sometime soon after.

One evening, when Tatiana had asked about Jessie at the dinner table, Conrad had sneered, "That black girl, Jessie never held me in proper esteem; she was rude to me once. I got rid of her."

Conrad didn't finish the whole story about Jessie when he had been at the office with her working overtime a week earlier. He usually told Tatiana, and others, only the part of a story that inflated his own ego. He never, ever, told the whole story, and always embellished his part of the tale so that he would look good.

"Poor Jessie. Nice, young lady from Tennessee, needed a good job up here," Tatiana said sadly as she kissed Charlotte and put her in her bed.

"Yes, we had to let Jessie go. Poor lady, black or whatever. She never was one of us. From the deep south, she was. Wore hand-me-down clothes from her older sister, I heard. Hands that were chapped and nails broken from working in her vegetable garden and washing dishes in a café on weekends, others told me."

Tatiana poured her husband another glass of the more expensive Pinot Noir that only he was allowed to drink. "Yes, poor Jessie. That office position was the best-paying work she'd ever had in Canada. It paid for her poor father's nursing home, as well as her basement suite rent, Conrad, my dear."

Conrad stuck his nose deep into the wine glass and smelled the bouquet. "Well, she was ill-mannered and disrespectful, especially to your husband. Never learned good manners from her people down there, never brought me a cup of coffee, and never stood up when I entered her small office to give her a completed sale contract to copy," Conrad complained as he got up and poured his wife a glass of cheap, white house wine.

After a quiet evening meal, Tatiana got up and took Conrad's empty dinner plate. She brushed off some dandruff from his shoulder and cleaned his chin of the apple pie she had baked for dessert. "Well, poor lady. I hope she finds another good job elsewhere. She liked working with the other women. Like a family she never had, she told me, Conrad," Tatiana added as she left.

Conrad slammed his fist down on the table. The remaining dishes rattled as he glowered at Tatiana. "Listen to me, woman. She told Flo, the other steno, that I was haughty, conceited, sought admiration, and was too self-important. 'Poor black lady,' indeed: she'll never amount to anything," he shouted, and added, "Is that what you think of your good husband?"

Tatiana cleaned up the wine spilled from Conrad slamming

the table. "Goodness gracious, of course not, Connie, er … sorry, Conrad. No, not at all. You're very generous to me: buying me that bicycle for Christmas, and a new vacuum cleaner, my sweet. Jessie should have had more respect for you," she said. She walked over to comfort Charlotte, who had woken up and cried out with her father's angry outburst.

Conrad swilled down another glass of Pinot Noir and slowly calmed down. "You're damn right she should have. More respect, as you rightly said." He got up and stomped out of the kitchen, ignoring baby Charlotte.

"Yes, more respectful."

"I have work to do: the newspapers need a first-class ad for that pricey condo I'll be putting on the market next week. The chief at the office told me that I'm the only agent that can write up such a glowing ad," he added. He showed her the ad he had started to write on his iPhone.

"Yes, you're good at that, Conrad. You're the best, Conrad. The one and only. Very, very well written, Conrad," she exclaimed, patting him on the back, adding, "Congratulations."

Conrad puffed up his chest. He went to the kitchen mirror, took out his comb, and brushed back his hair. He then opened his mouth and looked at his teeth, wet his finger and smoothed back his eyebrow. He stood there admiring his face, smiling and grinning, for a long time.

"I'll vacuum the living room carpet while you do your important work in the study, Conrad. I'll keep our baby quiet while you work," Tatiana said as she kissed Conrad on the cheek.

"Yes, I'll do that and keep that brat from howling," he growled. "The owner of the firm, Stratham agreed to give me my own office tomorrow. I'll tell you now, Tatiana, that I'm thinking of buying

Stratham out. Soon," he added, crowing, as he ushered Tatiana out to get her vacuum cleaner.

Tatiana stopped and looked bewildered. "But Conrad. Do we have the money? Mr. Stratham has been in business a long time. He's well respected in the community."

"Oh, don't you worry your pretty little blonde head about money. I know the bank manager and all about financing. Freddy Chan, the manager, he knows how much I bring in. He'll finance me. I could do better than Stratham. Getting old and feeble, he is."

Tatiana knew that she would worry her pretty little head, but she wasn't going to argue. She knew that Conrad had financed his new car through Mr. Chan. She saw the bank notes and contract on his desk. She was worried about money since she was pregnant again. She feared telling her husband; he'd told her that he didn't want any more children.

The next morning, Conrad was strutting about in the real estate office, reminding anyone and everyone who would listen how he had maneuvered the sale on that expensive property. He showed everyone the pictures of himself signing the contracts with the sellers.

Jackson Stratham came into Conrad's office, which he was sharing with Aziz, his younger associate. "You did well with that contract, Conrad. Well done," Stratham said as he pumped Conrad's hand a few times.

"Well, you owe me one, Jackson. Now, when do I get my own office? With a window that I can open to let some fresh air into this stale office," he brazenly asked, nodding toward Aziz contemptuously.

Mr. Stratham let out a stifled cough and hesitated with the insult. Aziz, a newcomer who was mentored by Conrad, squirmed and got up to leave the embarrassing conflict that was about to transpire.

"That office with the window has been occupied by my son. He's done well, also. I'll have to wait for another office to come open, Conrad. Won't be long."

Conrad bristled, the hair on his nape standing up. "Well, Jackson. I'm selling more than your son, and I'm now the best in the firm. I deserve a better percentage of my sales, also. Flo said that the books reveal such is the state of affairs around here."

"I know that Flo, my niece, and others here see you as being the biggest earner. She told me at our family dinner that you are talented, and we all recognize that you are unique in your powers of persuasion, Conrad."

Conrad poked his finger at Stratham's chest and continued to gloat. "Flo is a bright lady. Bright lady, your niece. I taught her how to manage those accounting books and how to organize her desk better."

"Maybe so, Conrad, but she had no business revealing to you our accounts and bank statements. That's my business. Not yours," Stratham said and walked away.

Conrad went to him and pulled him back roughly. "Listen, Jackson. I'm ready to buy this agency out. What's your price? I could do better."

Stratham kept his cool, smiled and answered, "Not for sale. Maybe you could do better in another real estate firm, Conrad. I heard that Preston and Whittaker across town are looking for good, high-powered agents."

"Maybe I should. Would be a big loss for this firm."

"I know that you already talked with Ross, the owner. You had no business telling Ross about my business affairs. Big mistake. Go see them tomorrow, and take your things with you. Flo will help you move," he said and walked away.

Conrad was stunned. He saw Aziz talking with the boss: they were both smiling. Conrad left and went to the local bar for a drink, fuming and planning how to get at his boss.

When he got home early, Tatiana greeted him with a peck on the cheek and asked, "Conrad, you're home early. Are you not well?"

Conrad shrugged, strutted about like a peacock, and puffed himself up to his full height of five-foot-six. "Nah, just need some quiet time to plan on meeting with Freddy Preston and Ross, the owner. He wants me to join his real estate firm."

"Oh, my gosh. How will we … ah … er … you … manage?"

Conrad waved her question aside. "He heard of my excellent work ethic and needed one of the best with lots of experience," he lied without blinking an eye.

Tatiana expressed some anxiety over their finances. She wanted to tell Conrad that her period was two months late. But she was quickly hushed up and barely reassured by Conrad, who stomped out. He ignored little Charlotte, who was playing with a rattle in her crib.

The next day, late in the afternoon, Conrad knew that the offices would be empty with all the agents out in the field. He walked into his workplace and found Flo in his office and Aziz sitting at his desk.

He was greeted by Flo, "Good afternoon, Conrad. I heard about your meeting with my uncle. Sorry to hear, but he told me to clean your desk out. I put everything in that box by the front door. You'll find everything in order, and I'll mail you your check at month's end."

Aziz was on the phone but waved goodbye to Conrad with a smile. Conrad gave Aziz the finger. Flo left and returned to her desk. Stratham's door was closed. Conrad left his office and walked by Flo's desk.

Flo looked up and said, "All the best." She added, "Good luck, Conrad, but I should tell you that your wife just phoned me a few minutes ago."

"She did? Tatiana? What the hell does she want now?"

Flo looked nervous as she replied, "Well, she said that she got your new car out of the service station for the lube and oil. Took all the money out of the joint bank account and drove Charlotte with her to move into a condo with Jessie. Jessie got a better job working with Preston and Whittaker."

Conrad was stunned, but quickly recalled that his first wife had done the same. "Bitch," was all he said.

He quickly composed himself, turned, and winked at Flo. "So, how about you and me go out for a nice drink and dinner after you're finished today? Celebrate my big real estate deal last week."

"Oh, love too, big guy. I'll be finished by five."

"This big guy will see you at five," he said, smirking.

Conrad smiled to himself. He leaned over and gave Flo a peck on the cheek. He gathered his belongings at the door, but stopped to admire himself in the full-length mirror at the exit. He took out his iPhone and snapped a photo of himself.

Then he combed his hair, straightened out his tie, smiled at his image in the mirror, and walked out thinking of what could be with Flo after dinner and a few drinks.

"She'll be more than satisfied with this big guy," he mumbled to himself as he left the building.

NARCISSISTIC CHARACTERS

This word, narcissist, is derived from Greek mythology. Narcissus was a hunter and a very beautiful young man. While in the hills, he leaned over a pool of water to drink, but suddenly saw his reflection in the water. He immediately fell in love with his own image.

Thus, narcissists are known to fall in love with themselves at an early age.

Sigmund Freud and other analysts wrote papers about such narcissists. It was recognized then, and by many psychiatrists now, to be a character disorder. As such, it is considered to be a pervasive characteristic pattern of grandiosity and stateliness, in fantasy and in behavior. There is a need for admiration and a lack of empathy for others, as Conrad demonstrated when he related to his wife and others, in the above fiction story.

This disorder is present in a variety of contexts: in social situations, personal relationships, and throughout one's employment. Generally, it begins in early adulthood and remains constant throughout the years.

Basically, narcissists have an exaggerated sense of importance, and entitlement. They require constant admiration, as Conrad in the above fictionalized story always demonstrated. Conrad was preoccupied with fantasies of unlimited success, power, brilliance, beauty, and ideal love.

There have been a large number of such narcissists throughout history. Some historians have depicted Alexander the Great as a raging narcissist, as well as Henry VIII, who was charismatic and in constant need of power and recognition. Hitler's and Stalin's characters also displayed such. Some have suggested that pop idols such as Madonna and Lady Gaga have displayed such characteristics.

Again, as Conrad demonstrated, narcissists need to be recognized as superior and unique with exceptional talents. They are always preoccupied with fantasies of power and of great intelligence. They usually choose a mate who must comply and constantly extol on such virtues, as did Tatiana. He expected her to be dedicated only to him and constantly enhance his self-esteem, at the expense of their only child.

A narcissist's friends and family find that conversations are monopolized by this character, and they are taken advantage of in order for the narcissist to get what they want in recognition. Such a character is unwilling and unable to see the needs or feeling of others, and is often boastful, arrogant, haughty, and pretentious. They will insist on buying the best of cars and clothes and want the biggest office, as Conrad did.

At the same time, they unfortunately have interpersonal problems, react with rage if slighted, and belittle others to make themselves appear superior. With such internal demands in character, they are prone to stress and depression if their demands are not met. Secretly, they have feelings of insecurity, shame, and humiliation.

The cause of a narcissistic personality disorder, as with so many other character disorders, is basically very complex and poorly defined. Some authorities postulate that childhood experience is important, with excessive adoration or criticism from a parent. Genetics may be valid as a cause, but others suggest a neurobiological brain disorder.

It appears that the disorder affects males more than females, and it usually begins in the teenage years. Complications occur for such adults with relationship difficulties, problems in education, and in the workplace. Such great personal demands, if unmet, produce ensuing stress, anxiety, depression, and physical health problems. Due to such stress, alcohol or drug addiction and potentially suicidal thoughts or behavior may follow.

Many highly-successful individuals display personality traits that might be considered to be narcissistic. However, only when such traits are inflexible, maladaptive, and cause persisting, significant functional impairment and subjective stress to themselves or to others do they constitute a narcissistic personality disorder.

Treatment is very difficult, since such a character has a very poor understanding of their personality. They rarely come spontaneously for treatment. Usually, they appear for therapy with the family physician only when they finally suffer from stress that causes a physical problem like cardiovascular, respiratory, or gastrointestinal difficulties.

Depression or substance abuse addiction will also cause such an individual to seek treatment. Either that or when these medical and psychiatric conditions appear along with loss of employment or a relationship due to that character's pathological personality.

However, therapy with a registered counselor or with a qualified psychologist over a period of time can lead to a favorable outcome and prognosis, both for the personality aspects and the medical complications.

A referral to a psychiatrist may be necessary for the treatment of the anxiety, depression, or substance abuse problems that accompany the disorder. The appropriate medication may be required under the direction of that psychiatrist if other mental illnesses are recognized.

Family, partners, or friends may be involved individually for support and understanding, and group therapy could be very therapeutic. Counseling may also be therapeutic through a religious foundation.

JULIAN, THE PYROMANIAC

When I came out to the waiting room to invite Julian into my consultation room, I found him cuffed to a security officer. "Hi, Julian, I'm Doctor Warren," I said. I shook the officer's outstretched hand and added, "It's alright, officer. I'd like to speak with Julian alone in my office, please. He'll be okay with me."

The officer nodded, took out his keys, and freed Julian of his handcuffs. "We'll be about an hour, Julian," I said, but looked at the officer, who acknowledged the fact with a wave of his hand.

"My receptionist will get you a coffee, if you wish," I said as I pointed to Harriet, who returned a smile from the officer.

"Not just yet, Doctor. Maybe later, thanks."

Julian got up and followed me to my office. I saw him wink at Harriet as he passed by her desk. He continued to rub his wrists from the shackles.

I asked him in, closed the door behind us and told him to take a seat.

Julian abruptly stopped and surveyed the spacious office. "Wow, plush place, doc. Nice and spiffy. Two nice, comfy chairs near the window, doc. Which one?"

"Thanks, Julian. Whichever one you take, and I'll sit in the other one."

Julian was uncertain. I watched him debating which chair to use. He began to count quietly, pointed at each chair, and used his ten fingers to count methodically. He was very undecided.

It was clear to me that he had a compulsive disorder that prevented him from making a decision. "Take that one, Julian. Nice view of the mountains. I'll sit here," I offered, and I sat down in the other chair across from him.

He stood for another minute, finished counting on his fingers, brushed his blond hair back, licked his fingers, and sat down.

I had read the police report and the statement from his lawyer, who had referred Julian Campbell to me for a consultation. Prior to sentencing him, the judge wanted a psychiatric opinion to see if he was mentally ill in his history of setting fires.

Julian was thirty years old, single after living with a young girl for four years, whom he was now separated from. He was perhaps depressed looking, I thought, but athletic and in tip-top shape. Julian was well-groomed and in sporty, expensive jeans, pricey Nike runners, and a form-fitting, exclusive shirt that emphasized his muscular body in the tight jean jacket.

I looked at Julian, making good eye contact at first, but he looked away. "So, what's going on, Julian?"

He took his time, and I watched as he counted again using his fingers. "No notes? I never saw a real shrink before. That Harriet of yours … but, you know what I mean, she looks real swell."

"Yes, she does a very good job. Notes? Some psychiatrists do, but we'll just talk, Julian. No notes."

"Talk about what? Yeah, well, but the weather? What's your first name?"

"Roy. Doctor Roy Warren. No, not the weather: about you being arrested for fire-setting. Tell me about that, please."

He shook his head, and I saw him begin counting the number of diplomas I had above my desk, near the door. "Nothing to tell. You got five up there," he said as he pointed to the far wall and again counted the five slowly and one at a time.

Finally, he talked briefly about his fire-setting. "Not a big deal, doc. I liked to watch fires. Liked to see that shed I torched. Damned cops caught me watching that old, abandoned house in the neighborhood go up in flames."

That was it. He wasn't going to go any further at this point. I could see that he was resisting the topic of fires. "Okay, then. Where were you born, and what were your parents like, Julian?"

Julian hesitated. "My pa died when I was thirteen. Bad luck number, my ma said to me, thirteen, know what I mean? Blamed me for not being nice to my pa. Overdosed on coke and other junk. Not a nice man."

Was he looking sad? He had lost his father and, recently, his girlfriend. "Sorry to hear. So, are you depressed with those losses? What happened after that with your mother and you?"

"Yeah, it's a sad time for me, 'specially after my girl buggered off. Know what I mean? So, I looked after my younger sister. Ma left us with Uncle Igor. Lived in Weyburn with my aunt after that."

That was the extent of that. He stopped and waited as he looked out the window at the building across the street. Was he counting the windows on that building?

I waited, but nothing transpired. "How was Uncle Igor?"

Julian stopped to check his iPhone. I patiently waited while he texted a message. He finished and turned back to face me, making good eye contact for the first time. "Firefighter. But, well, chief fireman he was in that small town."

There was my opening about fire-setting. I took it. "Fireman? How did that affect you, Julian?"

Julian had his head down. Morose? Finally, he said, "Yeah, well, but my little sister died. Couldn't help her, either. Heart gave out, and you doctors couldn't find her a new one. Know what I mean? Died when I was seventeen. Rheumatic fever, they said. Seventeen. Bad luck number my Aunt Bessy said to me, she did."

Depressed for certain. Young sister, father, girlfriend. "Sorry to hear, again, Julian. How old was she?"

Poor Julian was depressed. Was he going to cry? "Fifteen. Rheumatic fever, they said. Fifteen. My favorite little sister, so do you get it?"

"I do, Julian. Yes, I do. You had another sister? Surely you had some close siblings?"

"Well, but, shit, no. And don't call me Shirley."

I waited until that sank in. "Okay, Julian."

"Uncle Igor used to take me to help put out fires. On his red fire truck, like, with a siren. Peachy keen."

"How did that make you feel? Was that helpful in dealing with your loss?"

Julian perked up, and a faint smile crossed his face. "Well, but yeah. Made me feel warm and cozy-like. Unlike Aunt Bessy. She was a cold, frigid one. So I moved to Vancouver. Alone. Know what I'm saying, doc?" He gave a dramatic shudder with his arms and shoulders, and added, "Bbbrrr, like. Know what I'm saying with Aunty Bessy?"

"Yes. So you would set fires to make you warm and cozy, I guess? You're depressed, are you, Julian?"

Julian began scratching at his right arm and he started to

blush. "How did you know, Smart ass?" he asked, hiding his face in his hands.

I ignored that. "You were tense, depressed with the loss of your little sister, blamed by your mother for your father's death, and had a cold, unaffectionate aunt. You lost your girlfriend. The fires you set were a relief? Nice and warm and cozy, and it cured you of your stress and sadness? But for a short while only?"

Julian nodded. He got up and walked about the room, pacing back and forth. "Smart ass," he said again. He looked at me, but couldn't control his blinking.

"Not really, Julian. It just made common sense. Were you ever feeling that people were against you? Ever hear voices talking to you? Ever take drugs?"

"Shit, no. Not going to be like my old man. My girlfriend was a good girl. Left me. Found out I was setting fires in the neighborhood. Told her mother, know what I'm saying? Shit."

That was enough for me. He wasn't psychotic. A pyromaniac. A character disorder, pure and simple. Well, not that simple, but a disorder. Only job left for me was to write a medical-legal report and then for the judge to decide.

"So tell me. How did they catch you?"

"Yeah, well, but Ron … you tell me. Who squealed? Maybe my frigging aunt, or Jocelyn, my ex-girlfriend. Friggin' bitch."

"It's Roy, not Ron. I doubt it: the police have their ways now, Julian. Surely you must have known that you'd get caught. Ah, sorry, not Shirley. Julian it is."

Julian was very curious as he sat down again. "Yeah, well, but how, Rob?"

"Should I tell him?" I thought quickly. Might not be a good idea, but I did. "Roy: it's Roy. The police sent out a plainclothes policewoman. It could be a male officer as well. They scan the crowd and watch for a younger male, usually somewhere near the back or on the sidelines."

Julian perked up and became very intense. "So, what the fuck for?"

He spat out his gum into his hand and stuck it to under the edge of his chair.

"So, they watch for a guy with an ecstatic but spaced-out look on his face. He may also be playing with himself in his pants. The fire is very seductive sexually, and it relieves a lot of stress and tension for the fire-setter."

Julian looked away and stared out the window for the longest time. "Yeah," was all he said, but quickly added as he pointed out my door, "That Harriet … how old is she? You know what I'm saying?"

I saw Julian's eyes light up as he asked about Harriet. "Not sure, in her fifties. Was it like that for you all the time when you set fires, Julian? Playing with your genitals and feeling nice, warm, and cozy?"

He was afraid to confess. He waited a long time, but finally came out with it. "Yeah. It was a woman copper. Asked me what I was doing. I zipped up my fly and she cuffed me. Shit … very embarrassing, Ron."

I presumed he kept missing my name on purpose because he was angry at me for being a 'smart ass.' "Are you annoyed with me? It's Roy. So, setting fires is a big relief for you. You're quite obsessive. Compulsive. Counting. Neat and tidy like. Well-organized."

Julian smiled finally. "Yeah, well, but that was what my school teacher said to me. So what are you going to tell that judge? That I'm angry?"

"None of the embarrassing stuff, Julian. Just a medical-legal letter saying that you were not insane—that is, psychotic—but an obsessive-compulsive pyromaniac. It's part of being that kind of a character disorder. It's treatable, if you're interested."

"Yeah, maybe. It was an abandoned building: no good to anyone. I only picked no-good sheds, garbage bins, and garages: empty ones and shit like that," he added. "They caught me at that abandoned house. That was a good fire," he chuckled. He was almost ecstatic, with a flushed face.

With that memory of the blazing fire, he was almost in a daze. His face was red, and his eyes were looking far off somewhere. I watched as he moved his hand down and began holding onto his crotch, which may have had a bulge in it.

"Julian, we'll have to stop here. I see that this memory of that fire was very exciting for you. You relived that experience, almost in a trance," I said in a calm, reassuring manner.

He only nodded and said nothing in response. Julian knew that this interview was finished. He got up and looked closely at my diplomas on the wall. He scanned the papers on my desk and the telephone.

Finally, he sat down again and fingered the chair, looking for his wad of gum. When he couldn't find it, he brought out his pack of cigarettes and lit up.

I offered him an ashtray from my desk as he watched the fire from his lighter for the longest time. Julian put his left hand over the flame and felt the warm glow.

"Bad habit, smoking: lethal for your respiratory system. The lungs, Julian."

He put the lighter away. "Good for my lungs, Roy. Nobody dies from this shit now."

"Well, we had a neighbor who died from his wife smoking in their house all day and night."

"No shit. Died from smoking?"

I waited. Should I tell him? "No, she was mad at him for complaining all the time about her bad habit. She shot him."

Julian didn't reply to that and only shrugged and mumbled incoherently. "That Harriet. Swell lady. Real swell. Know what I'm saying?" he asked, but quickly added with a snicker, "So, if I told her that she had a beautiful figure, would she hold it against me?"

For a quick second I wasn't sure how to reply. But I reverted back to Psychiatry 101, and answered, "Well, I think we should really focus on you, Julian. We can talk about you some more the next time, if we meet again."

"Okay, Ron. Sorry, Roy. Yep, like as I said, you were okay, also. Not as bad as I first thought. Know what I'm saying?"

"Yes, I do. Thanks, Julian. By the way, it's Roy, my name: you got it right," I said as I opened the door and ushered Julian out. Once in the waiting room, we found the officer and Harriet chatting about his work on the police force.

The officer set his empty coffee cup on the receptionist's desk and put the cuffs back on Julian.

"All the best to you, Julian. Take care of yourself, and see the prison psychiatrist for therapy, Julian; or when you get out, maybe on parole. They will help you."

The officer ushered Julian to the door. "Thanks Roy," Julian said as they walked away. Julian turned slightly, smiled, and winked at Harriet. She smiled back.

I went back to my consultation room and dictated the independent medical examination report on my recorder for my receptionist to type out.

I concluded that he was not suffering from a serious mental illness, and was a personality disorder: a pyromaniac, and that was serious, but treatable. I recommended parole, but only if he agreed to psychotherapy. I said that I'd be willing to treat him if the judge agreed to parole and that progress reports for the court would follow regularly.

A month later, I heard from Julian's lawyer. The judge had agreed and done as I'd suggested at the sentencing trial, but with strict conditions on his behavior, including frequent meetings with a parole officer and reports on his progress from me.

I concluded that it was cheaper for society to pay for a psychiatrist than the expense of incarceration in prison.

Julian came to see me a week after seeing that judge. He agreed to meet with me every two weeks, which included a mild prescription for his stress and obsessive disorder. I added a very mild anti-depressant for his depression with his multiple losses.

He resisted setting fires, the parole officer informed me regularly. Julian had also found a nice girlfriend. "She told me that she loved me despite my bad past history. She's going to move in with me soon, I hope," he said as I made notes.

He got my name right each time, but I think he came mostly to visit that "swell girl" in the front office.

I knew what he meant.

PYROMANIACS

Pyromania is often used interchangeably with the term arson, but the two behaviors perpetrated by specific character disorders are vastly different. Arsonists, like Gilbert in the first fictionalized story, set fires for monetary or vindictive reasons—that is, simply to make money or get revenge. Pyromaniacs suffer from an impulse character disorder and set fires because they are unable to resist the destructive impulse.

Usually, that impulse is the result of an uncontrollable need to deal with some overwhelming mental state, like rage, stress, anxiety, or depression. Thus, the pyromaniac attempts to cope with their psychiatric condition by fire-setting. The arsonist commits a criminal act, but is also basically a character-disordered individual who may be paid to destroy a building.

The desire and need for a pyromaniac to set fires may start in puberty, and males are statistically in the majority. Such a person has an uncontrollable urge to set fires and has a fascination with and attraction to fires and fire-setting paraphernalia such as matches, lighters, etc.

A pyromaniac has a tension and excitement around the thought of, or the specific action of, setting a fire. They enjoy a pleasure, excitement, or rush, followed by relief after they watch the conflagration.

Such individuals may make considerably long preparations in the planning and setting of the fire. They are also indifferent to the consequences to life or property caused by the fire, and will only derive satisfaction from the resulting destruction.

Again, pyromaniacs are mostly males, usually with poor social skills and possibly with intellectual difficulties.

The setting of fires by a pyromaniac may be the result of terrorist activity, concealing a crime, making a political statement, or attracting attention or recognition for some cause. It may also be an isolated act during a bipolar mental state or other such serious mental condition, or while under the influence of drugs or alcohol.

The cause, as with other character disorders, is basically unknown. Some postulate childhood abuse, genetics, intellectual and social deficits, addictions, and other mental health conditions. Many suggest that it provides a certain sexual urge for males who are unable to form meaningful romantic relationships.

Some have considered certain rock & roll bands to be pyromaniacal by using fire, flames, and other incendiary devices as a pyrotechnical display while performing. In the mid-1960s, the famous band *The Who* packed a drum with explosives to make an unforgettable bang. It had such huge, inflammatory effect that a band member's hair was singed and another injured.

The complicated and lengthy procedure of preparing the location and setting the fire is a gradually exciting pleasure, which may be purely sexual in nature. Being present and observing the fire itself becomes a sexual release for such an offender.

Apart from a sexual release, some pyromaniacs also have a release of other internal emotional conflicts during preparation and observation. For example, the overwhelming stress while suffering from other maladies like depression, anxiety, guilt, or other interpersonal distress problems is relieved by the process.

They are usually discovered at the scene while in sexual ecstasy, or in another obvious state of mental despair, and are then arrested and charged by the police. The courts will then suggest a psychiatric opinion for an evaluation of that perpetrator's mental state.

Treatment, as with other character disorders, is very difficult since such a character has very poor insight into their personality. Pyromaniacs rarely come forward spontaneously for treatment. Usually, they appear for therapy with the family physician, but only when they suffer from stress that causes a physical problem like cardiovascular, respiratory, or gastrointestinal difficulties. That physician, if aware, may then refer the patient for psychiatric therapy.

Depression or substance abuse addiction may also cause the pyromaniac to seek treatment. Such medical and psychiatric conditions may appear with loss of employment, a relationship, or other crisis.

However, therapy with a registered counselor or with a qualified psychologist over a period of time can lead to a favorable outcome and prognosis, both for the personality aspects and the medical complications.

A referral to a psychiatrist may be necessary for the treatment of the anxiety, depression, or substance abuse problems that accompany the disorder. The appropriate medication may be required under the direction of that psychiatrist.

The family, partner, or friends of the pyromaniac may be involved individually for support and understanding, both with individual cognitive therapy with a qualified psychologist or counselor, or with group therapy.

FRANCISCO, THE EXHIBITIONIST

"Listen, Francisco, that is your sixth beer now. Take it easy, buddy. Good to celebrate your thirtieth big day, but you're the one driving, remember?" Hernando, his good buddy, cautioned. He was aware of what was going to transpire.

Francisco shifted slightly in his aisle seat, as the weather was hot for early August in Regina, Canada, and he was sweating in anticipation of running out on the football field naked. "It will be warm enough in this open stadium," he whispered to Hernando.

"If you are caught again then you will go to jail for certain, my friend."

Francisco shrugged his athletic shoulders and only nodded in agreement. He'd made certain that the two of them had seats close to the field and that he was in the aisle seat, where he could easily vacate at the right moment. "Too hot for me, Hernando. Needed to sit here so that I could cool down with a few cool ones," Francisco joked.

Hernando didn't think it funny; he was wise to his friend and knew what might happen quite soon. After all, he had admonished him years ago, and on occasion gotten him out of jail in other cities over the past few years for running about naked in sports stadiums.

"Listen, mi amigo. You are not to expose yourself to my two younger sisters again. You hear? They were shocked to see you with all that hanging out when you walked into their bedroom," he had admonished his friend last week.

"Okay, okay. They needed a lesson in male anatomy," Francisco had laughed.

Hernando knew that the same activity would occur again today on the field. Especially after all that booze that he'd consumed.

Francisco put his sixth empty down on the floor with the rest of the bottles. He knew that it would be quick and easy to doff his jacket and slacks and shake off his sandals at the bottom of the aisle. The door to the field could be opened easily once he was ready.

"You're in the way, buddy boy. Can't see my winning team get off the field. Wanna watch the band and the good-looking cheerleading girls get on," the older man standing behind Francisco shouted at him.

"It won't be long, buddy boy," Francisco yelled back as he stripped off his jacket, slipped off his slacks, and threw away his sandals. He turned to fully expose himself to the crowd of young women, older men, and teen girls sitting behind him in the Taylor Field football stadium.

Hernando threw up his arms when he saw his buddy wiggle his pelvis and shake himself in front of the crowd. He yelled out, "Get back here, estúpido. You'll be arrested again."

Francisco just laughed as the older women gasped, the younger teens gaped and screamed, and many men just hooted, hollered, and urged him on. He walked to the gate, opened it, and ran onto the field.

This was just as the young cheerleaders marched onto the center of the field to do their dance.

Many in the crowd began to march up the stands and out for a beer, but turned and began to laugh and shout. They all encouraged Francisco as he ran around the perimeter stark-naked, waving to the crowd as his genitals rocked back and forth.

As he trotted about, he could see stadium security and three of the Regina police chasing after him. He heard the cheerleader's manager yell out, "Let's all of us just circle around and huddle up. We don't know what that crazy will do."

Francisco was a good runner, and easily outran the security guards and the three local police officers who were called in. "Hold up there, man. We're going to catch you and off to jail you go. Have some decency. Young girls here, mister," one of the officers shouted as he tried to get close to Francisco.

Francisco evaded the police and circled the cheerleaders, who were huddled together. He stopped occasionally to wiggle his pelvis in front of the dumbfounded young girls. "Never seen some of these good-sized ones before, ladies?" he shouted as a few of the girls put their hands over their eyes and covered their faces.

A few shouted heartily and laughed at him. This just got him more excited to watch the shock on some of the girl's faces when he stopped in front of them.

It was that mistake when the police finally surrounded him. The three of them wrestled him to the turf as the crowd in the stands whistled and hollered, "Get him coppers." Others shouted, "Better show than our team: let him go, let him go."

As he lay there, he was pleased to see many of the cheerleaders looking down on him as they gasped in horror at his nakedness. This immediately brought the memory of his two older sisters as they gaped in horror when he walked into their bedrooms as a young boy, wildly flaunting his nakedness.

He recalled that he hadn't been rebuked by his parents with that activity. After all, they were both nudists and often walked about naked. In his late teens he often joined them at the nudist colony in San Diego, California after the family had moved there from Mexico.

Francisco was cuffed by the police just as his friend, Hernando, met them at the gate, where he was allowed to dress. At the local police station he was charged with exhibiting himself, fined, and given a court date to appear before a judge.

"This is your fourth offence, young man, as I see from your police records from Montréal," the judge said, glaring down at him from his bench. "I'll put you on probation, but it's jail the next time," he added sternly and slammed his gavel down.

That was when, the next day, he and his friend packed their meager goods and drove to Vancouver. He was unaware of the police warrant on his head for evading his parole date.

In Vancouver, Francisco got a job as a lifeguard at a local private community club where he could flaunt his dark, athletic Mexican body to the admiring older women. However, he gradually became depressed when one of the girls from the club whom he was dating rejected him after two months of an intense physical relationship.

"She objected to me always walking about in the nude in her condo with her blinds up, standing in front of the window with the people passing by. Called me a pervert, Hernando," he told his friend at breakfast in the basement suite that they both rented in the downtown city core.

"Well, I remember you doing the same in San Diego, California when our parents moved from Mexico, Francisco," Hernando said in sympathy, looking at his despondent friend.

Francisco was glum and silent but said, "I thought it was the normal thing to do. Remember? My parents joined that local nudist club, and my mother would make tacos and burritos in the kitchen with everything hanging out. My papa never was dressed, and they ate with nothing on."

"That was also when you walked in on my older sister when she was in the shower. You were just totally naked, and she screamed for you to get out. My parents kicked you out of the house."

Francisco didn't tell his friend that he'd gotten so sexually excited thinking and planning the act that time with Hernando's sister in the shower. It was the astonished look on her face, the screaming and yelling that he enjoyed so much. It relieved his anxiety and despair in failing his high school exam that year.

However, he did confide in his friend that he was depressed. "You know, mi amigo, with my father's birthday today and my recent thoughts of his suicide by drug overdose, I am very unhappy. He made a big mistake to take the heroin, cocaine, and fentanyl all together."

"You must take those anti-depressants that your doctor prescribed before you go to work today, Francisco. I also saw that you are very angry to lose your good father," Hernando said as he too left for work that morning.

It was the next day after that conversation with his friend that Francisco exposed himself on the local bus. He was still furious at his father, and he refused to take his meds as prescribed. He was going to work at the club and recognized two young teenaged girls, Susan and Laura, on the bus who used the pool at the club.

He nodded and smiled at them and then sat across from them. They both giggled and waved at him in greeting. As he sat he slowly spread out his newspaper on the bus to cover his pelvis in front of the two teenaged girls.

While they were talking and giggling, he slowly unzipped his fly and opened his genitals, still covered by the newspaper. He looked about and was pleased that the three of them were alone at the back of the bus. When they looked at him coughing out loud he suddenly put the newspaper aside and openly revealed himself to them.

Susan gaped at his swollen member and immediately put her hands over her eyes, shouting, "Pervert. You're the swim coach at the club. I know you: you are a frigging perv."

Laura was more composed. She stood up, jammed the newspaper down, and then slapped Francisco across the face. She yelled out to the driver to call the police.

"Their shouts of horror were what stopped the bus. The driver came to me as two other passengers held me and the police arrested me again, Hernando," he told his friend in the jail cell.

It was three weeks later that Francisco was sent to the provincial prison with a sentence of two years, less a day. The judge stared down at him from her bench and also looked at his lawyer, Miss Lagosian.

"We have the documents from Regina, where you were under a warrant, Mister Francisco Vallarta. With that history of exhibitionism, I sentence you to two years, where you are to enter psychiatric treatment with Doctor MacPherson, the prison psychiatrist," she charged and slammed down her gavel, dismissing any further defense remarks that Miss Lagosian might have had.

Hernando often visited his friend at the prison. They talked about the good old days in Mexico and how their families had gotten work in southern California. "The prison shrink wants to talk with you, my friend. Said that I was unresponsive to his therapy and the fucking meds he gave me," Francisco said glumly. He got up and walked away, despondent.

Hernando spoke to the guards who escorted him to see the psychiatrist in his office on the main floor. The doctor had some time that late morning and was pleased to meet Francisco's friend.

"We have a good hour, Hernando, so make yourself comfortable in that chair. Thank you for agreeing to see me," Dr. MacPherson said as he pointed to the chair across from his desk.

After a few pleasantries, the psychiatrist explained, "Your good friend is seriously depressed, Hernando. He was angry at his father and very depressed, and was on some drugs when he exposed himself on that bus. His thoughts of doing so, and his plan to set out how to do it, and then the exhibitionistic act itself, were therapeutic actions that gave him relief."

"Yes, he often told me that his exhibitionism helped him with all his pent-up emotions. The planning gave him some relief."

"What was his anger all about?" MacPherson asked as he made notes.

Hernando thought for a minute. He wasn't sure how much to tell on his friend, but finally did explain, "His parents were nudists when he was a young boy. Mother still is. She left his father and my friend when he was still a young boy, and he never got over that loss."

"Is she still in touch with him? See him?"

"Hell no—oops, sorry. No. She returned to Mexico and joined a lesbian nudist colony in Acapulco."

"Oh?"

"Yep, shacked up with a very wealthy, Danish, older lesbian, and they live together in this lady's mansion in the hills above

Acapulco. Sad story, but she is very happy with her lifestyle now."

"The father. He died, your friend said of a coronary?"

"Hell no. Oops, sorry. No. Became addicted to drugs when his wife ran away. Lost his job. Never saw Francisco, but overdosed on fentanyl and other shit. Sorry, other drugs: heroin and coke," he said sadly.

"Sad, indeed. Francisco's exhibitionism is a cathartic action, a liberating, cleansing, purifying activity. I'll keep him on the anti-depressants and see him weekly for psychotherapy. He'll get better," the doctor said as he made some more notes and stood up.

The meeting was over.

"Get better? I sure hope so, Doctor. Sure hope so," Hernando said as he got up and walked to the office door. "He's my good buddy," he added as he turned and left.

It was only that following week that he learned that his good buddy had attempted suicide by hanging himself in his jail cell.

"It was late at night, Hernando. He cut up his bed sheets to make a rope. Good thing his cellmate woke up in time and saved him," Dr. MacPherson sadly told Hernando on the phone.

"He doesn't have many good friends. I never agreed with his unlawful activity of exhibiting himself, but he's still a good friend. I'll come and see him tomorrow."

"Yes. Please do. He could use a good friend at this time with his depression," the psychiatrist said as he hung up the phone.

EXHIBITIONISM

Exhibitionists are one of the personality disorders listed in the Diagnostic and Statistical Manual of Mental Disorders. Such character disorders are rare, but they act out by unlawfully exposing their genitals, either socially or in a private situation, often to younger girls.

The diagnostic criteria is such that a person, over a period of at least six months, has recurrent and intense sexual arousal from the exposure of one's genitals to an unsuspecting person, as manifested by fantasies, urges, or behaviors.

Such an individual may be aroused by exposing their genitals only to prepubescent children, only to physically mature individuals, or to both. A careful, detailed history of the type of activity, as just explained, must be understood to rule out a pedophilic character disorder that might require a different approach for therapy.

Exhibitionists often describe multiple mental disorders such as anxiety, anger, episodic rage, panic, or depression. They may resort to alcohol or drug addiction to allay such emotions. Many find that the fantasies, urges, the planning of the action or performing the action is an immediate temporary release for their mental disorder.

Exhibitionism is a public or semi-public (i.e. partly hidden) action of parts of the body where those anatomical parts are not normally exposed. For example, the breasts, genitals, or the buttocks of either sex. By law it is considered indecent exposure and can be prosecuted in a court.

Such a practice is a desire or compulsion, as Francisco demonstrated in the above fiction story. It becomes a desire to shock, usually, the other sex for their amusement or for that character's sexual satisfaction.

Historically, such behavior dates back thousands of years. There are such accounts of women flashing and baring their breasts and laws in England hundreds of years ago that made public nudity unlawful, subject to arrest and severe punishment.

In this day and age, the access to new technologies such as smart phones and tablets allows such behavior to be very prevalent, and usually beyond the law. It has allowed anyone to exhibit themselves openly, especially with nude selfies.

The term 'exhibitionist' was first coined by a French physician Lasegue in 1877. Subsequently, it was accepted as an action with a non-consenting person to the point that such a character has difficulties in his quality of life.

Men are twice as likely to exhibit the behavior than do women. Some women, however, have been accused of such behavior, socially or within their employment, by wearing revealing garments that are considered to be flagrantly exhibitionistic by others.

There are now very well-described instances of different types of exhibitionistic acts by women in society. For example, the lifting of skirts by women, baring their breasts, or, more rarely, the flashing of their genitals. Males are more prone to having others watch a sexual act, mooning (where buttocks are exposed), streaking as Francisco demonstrated, making obscene telephone calls, or exposing themselves to young, teenaged youth or children.

Streaking is not uncommon now in sporting arenas, again as the above fiction story demonstrated. It can be a prank or a dare, a form of protest, or a means of producing shock, which then may allay that person's inner emotional or mental disorder for a brief time.

It has become more common now for streakers to run amok down public avenues or for adults to march in the nude as a protest again government actions. Students at some colleges and universities have taken to expose themselves in marching or bicycle riding, again as a demonstration, which is then promoted in newspapers and on television.

Treatment of exhibitionists, as with other character disorders listed earlier, can be very difficult. They are usually apprehended and charged by the police. The courts will then suggest a psychiatric opinion for an evaluation of that culprit's mental state.

They rarely appear for therapy in the family physician's office. If they do, it is because of cardiovascular, respiratory, or gastrointestinal difficulties caused by stress. That physician, if aware of the underlying history, may then refer the patient for psychiatric therapy.

Depression, other mental conditions, alcoholism, or substance abuse addiction may also lead such an individual to seek treatment. The loss of employment or of a relationship may precipitate any of these medical or psychiatric conditions, and may in turn lead to therapy. However, the underlying cause, and exhibitionism, may not be revealed.

Therapy with a registered counselor or with a qualified psychologist over a period of time can lead to a favorable outcome and prognosis, both for the personality aspects and the medical complications.

A referral to a psychiatrist may be necessary for the treatment of the anxiety, depression, or substance abuse problems that accompany the disorder. The appropriate medication may be required under the direction of that psychiatrist.

The exhibitionist's family, partner, or friends may be involved individually for support and understanding, both alongside individual cognitive therapy with a qualified psychologist or counselor or with group therapy.

HUMPHREY, A TYPICAL SOCIOPATH

After leaving The Crimson Door with Siegfried, his drinking companion, Humphrey sat outside on a wooden bench and snorted a line of cocaine. "That girl, Ingrid, she called herself, was a real hot pole dancer, Siggy. Nice long legs and big boobs." Humphrey laughed as he blew his nose into his hand and wiped it onto his jeans.

"You took her into the back room for a quickie. How much did you give her for that quick poke?" Siegfried asked as he unbuckled his jacket. "Frigging hot, this weather you have in July. Not like my Frankfurt that I left last week," he added wiping his brow with his sleeve.

Humphrey chortled. "Are you kidding me? Bugger all. She asked for two big ones, but I told her I had to go to the ATM machine, and I'd be right back."

"That's why you were in such a rush to leave, I guess. I didn't even finish my beer."

It was just at that point that the older man came out and pointed his finger at Humphrey. He became belligerent as he put his hand on Humphrey's shoulder. "You owe me two hundred. Ingrid told me you used your dick and on her and didn't fork over the cash. Ready to run, were you?"

The older man, Solomon, was well into his sixties. He was the strip joint manager and the banker for the girls. He was not as well-muscled as Humphrey who, at age forty, was in good shape: brawny, quick on his feet and fast with his fists.

Humphrey recognized Solomon, who was also the one playing the piano while Ingrid danced naked. He got up and pulled the man's hand away. "Bugger off, you old crock. I'll be back next week to pay you," Humphrey said with a sneer on his face.

The man didn't flinch and spat at Humphrey, "We close an hour after midnight, so fork it over, motherfucker."

Humphrey wiped the man's spittle off his jean jacket. "You are harassing and assaulting a long-time customer," he said. He leaned back and punched the old man square in the face.

The old man fell to the ground. His nose was bleeding and he howled in pain, writhing on the pavement. Several street hookers and their pimps watched close by, but did nothing. They all knew Humphrey to be a mean hustler with a short temper.

"He spat at me. You saw that Siggy: he started that fight by assaulting me with his spit," Humphrey said to his buddy and shouted to the onlookers, who backed off.

With Solomon threatening to call the cops, Humphrey pulled his friend away and walked off. He saw the old man calling 911 on his mobile.

They were both running down the back alley, laughing as they heard the siren wailing nearby. "Gotta go, buddy. Going to Poland early in the morn. You sure screwed that Ingrid broad in more ways than one. See you in two weeks," Siegfried said, laughing as he walked away.

"Buying sausages and all that garlic for the restaurants in town, Siggy?"

"And for Olga, my wife," Siegfried said as he ran off.

Humphrey waved to his buddy. He felt safe enough in the lane, which was full of homeless people, hookers, pimps, and drug addicts sleeping off the booze or the drugs.

As he walked into the next lane across the street, he spotted a woman sleeping in the alley next to a large, blue garbage bin. He looked around. She was alone, huddled up in an old blanket with her skirt just covering her naked thighs.

"You awake, good looker? Still asleep on all that shit?" Humphrey asked, pushing her by the shoulder.

She didn't flinch and only mumbled something incoherent.

He pulled up her skirt over her belly and unzipped his jeans. "Not wearing any underwear, sweetie. Nice," he said as he pulled her legs apart and entered her.

When he was finished, he wiped himself off on her skirt and rolled her over onto her side. "Sleep tight, bitch. Almost as good as Ingrid, honey. At least she enjoyed it, bitch," he growled, kicked her in the buttocks, and walked away.

Humphrey laughed out loud to himself as he spotted a car in the lane. He was still sexually excited from thinking of that young Ingrid, a late teenager, he was sure. "Probably getting coke from Solomon, who also keeps half of what she earns. I would," he said to himself as he looked in the parked car.

The car was a newer BMW, and he spotted a black case inside with a laptop half-covered by a large ream of business papers. Again, he checked to see that he was alone. He then found a large, red brick close by. It took several quick blows to smash the rear window.

As the security alarm wailed, he snatched the laptop and the case and fled across the street. He checked the case and threw the papers aside onto the street but kept the laptop.

Two days later he called Olga. "No, he's on the plane to Warsaw," she answered in a hurry and hung up.

It was that very evening that Humphrey knocked on Olga's door in her and Siegfried's posh condo.

"Evening, Olga, my sweet. Look what good old Humphrey brought just for you and me," he said with a grin as he flashed two bottles of expensive rye whiskey and a plastic bag of cocaine.

Olga was expecting Humphrey; she knew him well and was sure he would come to see his good friend's wife. He whistled at her figure and the way she was dressed as he walked in. She was wearing a sheer housecoat, barely covering her hips and breasts, that was hardly held together by the open top.

Humphrey gave her a big hug as he squeezed her bottom. He made himself at home in the living room as they drank the rye whiskey, which she liked, and snorted the cocaine, which she loved. "You can stay the week, you hard motherfucker," Olga cooed in his ear as she pulled off his pants.

After all the wine and coke Olga was fast asleep on the couch next to him. He moved her over, spread her legs apart and helped himself again.

While she slept, snoring softly, he walked into her bedroom and rifled through Siegfried's closet and checked all his drawers. Two pairs of cufflinks, a spare Rolex watch, and several pieces of Olga's jewelry were too tempting to leave behind.

"Siggy is always losing his watches, and Olga has too much jewelry to miss," he said and smiled to himself. He joined Olga on the couch again after hiding his stolen hoard in his coat's inner pockets.

Humphrey left after five days. He feared his good buddy might come home early. "See you again soon, beautiful," he said, kissing her breasts.

"Yes, big guy. My Siggy goes to Hungary next week to buy that salami shit for the local cafes," she said as Humphrey fingered her from behind while they both stood at the door.

Olga almost feinted in ecstasy as she whispered in his ear, "He'll be gone for two weeks next time, big guy. Can you get away? How's that job of yours?"

"Aha, good you asked. I'm the manager now at that high-tech shop. Got twenty under me. Big salary increase," he lied, looking her in the eye. He wasn't going to tell her that he was fired three weeks ago for petty theft and then accused of rape.

That accusation was from a young oriental girl, an aide in the small firm, whom he had followed into the ladies restroom and wrestled to the floor.

With the loss of his work, and now before the courts, Humphrey needed money. He already knew what buildings in the west end of the city were lax in closing their gates after tenants parked their cars in the underground garage.

He waited outside that dark night, close by in the alley. He watched a silver Audi SUV click the remote and enter as the gates opened. He slid in before the gate came down. He took out his hammer, sharply-pointed screwdriver, and small bar and went to work on several cars.

Humphrey destroyed the windows on the cars or jimmied open the doors with the bar. He worked quickly and retrieved cameras, several laptops, some loose money, expensive jackets, parcels, and anything else worth money that he could exchange.

He used one of the cars' remotes to let himself out and was gone before anybody came in response to the car safety alarms blaring out. That next day, he pawned off all the stolen goods for close to a thousand dollars, together with Siegfried's watch, cufflinks, and multiple pieces of Olga's jewelry.

In those two weeks, Humphrey avoided Siegfried. "Got the flu, good buddy. Got to stay in bed," he lied on the phone to his 'good buddy.' He wouldn't see Olga again, as she had accused him of theft.

"Lots of other skirts with nicer pussies around here, Olga," he swore at her as he hung up.

In those two weeks, Humphrey was depressed with the loss of Olga and being poverty-stricken again. His rent was due, and he owed money to the few friends that he still had. He got into fights with door men at local bars, drank heavily, snorted cocaine with his friends in the downtown east side, and robbed two jewelry stores of all the money in their tills, flashing his stolen pistol at the Persian shop owners.

Unfortunately for Humphrey, he was also complaining of painful urination with a constant sliming, pussy discharge from his penis.

It was a doctor at a walk-in medical clinic who diagnosed the gonorrhea. "Your name, here, on the form you filled out is Albright? Jonas? Well, sorry to tell you Mister Jonas Albright. It's also called the clap," Dr. Valerie Constantine said to Jonas as she wrote out a prescription of an antibiotic for him. "Have you a wife, girlfriend? Partner, maybe?" she asked.

"Naw, but I'll use a condom when I'm with my young Peruvian doctor friend. He'll understand," he lied with a sneer on his face. He walked out, swearing to himself and calling that girl in the alley some time ago a bitch. Should he call the other women he'd had? he wondered.

He wasn't going to bother.

He was sure the antibiotic would work by the time he saw Olga again. She had already called him for the following weekend. He wouldn't tell his good buddy, Olga's husband, what Dr. Constantine diagnosed, either.

"Olga told me that he's impotent, anyway. Poor shmuck," he said to himself, laughing.

An image of the young Oriental aide, sobbing on the bathroom floor after his assault came to his mind. "She'll find out soon enough about the clap. Serves her right for laying that assault charge on me." He snickered.

ANTISOCIAL PERSONALITY DISORDERS

The essential feature of an antisocial personality disorder is a pervasive pattern of disregard for, and violation of, the rights of others, which begins in childhood or early adolescence and continues into adulthood.

This pattern has also been referred to as psychopathy, sociopathy, or dissocial personality. As with Humphrey in the above fiction story, deceit and manipulation are quintessential. Usually the presence of these features needs to be explained by friends, family, or other sources once the individual is apprehended, since they are not very forthcoming or honest in a psychiatric evaluation.

Sociopaths are occasionally able to form emotional attachments, as they are quite likeable with their outlandish lifestyle. However, they are unlike psychopaths, who are also usually charming and manipulative, but are often well-educated and capable of holding steady jobs.

Generally, the psychopath is deceitful and manipulative in social circumstances, but is rarely in conflict with the law. Humphrey demonstrated his illegal and unlawful tendencies, making him a sociopath or antisocial character. Generally, if the diagnosis is to be made it requires the subject's age to be at least eighteen and have a history of much unlawful activity.

The highest prevalence of such antisocial disorders is found mostly in males with drug or alcohol addiction, those who are in prisons, or other forensic settings. Prevalence is also highest in men affected by adverse socioeconomic conditions (e.g. poverty) or sociocultural factors (e.g. migration).

Antisocial or sociopathic characteristics are generally much more common in males than in females. It is possibly less diagnosed in females due to the lack of aggressive tendencies in women.

The diagnosis is made based on the observation that the antisocial character has a disregard for and violates the rights of others. This is indicated by a failure to conform to social norms, and lawful behavior, often leading to frequent arrests. Lying, the use of aliases, or the conning of others for personal pleasure or profit is very common.

Antisocial characters are impulsive, unable to plan ahead, irritable, aggressive, and have a reckless disregard for the safety of themselves or others. Furthermore, they are consistently irresponsible, unable to maintain a consistent work place, or honor financial obligations. Finally, they show a lack of remorse in their ability to hurt others with their behavior.

One of the most famous sociopaths known in recent history was Bernie Madoff. Over two decades Madoff conducted one of the largest Ponzi schemes in history. He defrauded people out of tens of billions of dollars and spent his remaining years in prison.

It is vital to make the diagnosis of antisocial personality apart from such behavior that may occur during other severe mental disorders such schizophrenia, bipolar disorder, while on drugs or alcohol, or suffering from a senile or traumatic brain disorder. During such disorders, the individual may act out in an antisocial manner, but only during that irrational episode.

Once again, as with other character disorders outlined, treatment can be very problematic. Such antisocial characters are usually only introduced to therapy when apprehended on several occasions, are before the courts, are referred by a lawyer, or are in prison.

Unfortunately, the prison system rarely has sufficient therapeutic capabilities to offer long-term therapy. However, treatment may be available in society through the family physician or with a religious pastor or similar mentor if such is qualified.

Psychological counseling with a qualified therapist may be very therapeutic on an individual basis or with group therapy. A psychiatrist may be involved for similar therapy, and medication may be necessary if overt emotional symptoms are evident.

The prognosis can be more favorable if friends, partners, or the family is involved. Such would encourage the individual to continue in treatment on a consistent, frequent basis and for a prolonged period of time.

Finally, it is imperative for the therapist to rule out the other possibilities for the behavior occurring, such as those other mental illnesses mentioned, especially in the organic, senile, or brain trauma injuries so commonly seen now in our society.

OLIVER, A HOMELESS MAN

Everybody always made fun of the old duffer, Oliver. Wherever he walked with his bad limp he was jeered, heckled, laughed at, or just punched in the back. He would be knocked over, allowing some of his goods to be stolen as he roamed the streets and back alleys. And all for no good reason.

"I guess that such is true because I'm darker, my face is weather-beaten and pock-marked from my chicken pox as a young kid, and probably because of my aboriginal heritage," he once told his old friend, Augustus, as he was urinating behind the tree on the corner.

He recalled that his mother, who left the family when he was only ten to live somewhere up north, told him, "Oliver, my boy, you also have some Scottish blood in them there veins of yours."

She went on as she packed her suitcase and was at the door, ready to catch the bus. Oliver was huddled in the corner of the one-room shanty, crying. She went on talking. "It was your great grandfather, I was told: name of MacKay, he was," his mother told him just before she left for Regina to find work.

Oliver later discovered that his mother had been taken from her family reserve in her late teens and sent to the government-run residential school in Regina. Joshua MacKay was the head principal there, and he had three children by his mother and several more by her girlfriends.

After she left, Oliver was cared for by several families in the northern area of Saskatchewan. Oliver never completed high school, and was addicted to drugs until he was incarcerated for several counts of theft.

While in jail, he learned how to repair cars—a trade he never used—but was clean of drugs thereafter. He moved from town to town, unemployed and depressed, until he settled in Vancouver in his late fifties. Or was he in his late sixties? He wasn't sure.

In the big city, no one knew his name, and no one cared. Many visitors and tourists along Hastings and Cordova just saw him to be a strange man, but always with a simple, vacuous smile.

His odd appearance was accentuated by his hunched-over gait, due to scoliosis of his back, as he shuffled along and pushed his cart. This odd shuffle, twitchy eyes, a nervous habit of constantly biting his lip, and scruffy, worn-out appearance was his usual persona known to the other homeless people in the area.

That was when he was living in the downtown east side of Vancouver, usually on the street in doorways or camped in his small, ratty tent in a park. But for his own safety he finally listened to his friend, "Good Time" Charlie. Good Time had come to visit Oliver one dark and stormy day at the tent park. He said, "Look here, Oliver, you need a safer place to sleep at night. Follow me. Let's get the Hell outta' here."

Oliver only nodded, packed his worldly goods, and walked with Good Time for over three miles. It was into a more well-established neighborhood, where it was less risky and out of the downtown area.

"The pickings are better in this area, Oliver. You can hustle the rich old ladies who go to the large grocery store nearby. Or, better still, wait for the rich dudes outside the bank as they deposit their money."

"Yeah, banks are good." Oliver smiled gleefully, rubbing his hands together.

"People always feel guilty for having money in the bank and will give you some of it. Cry a bit with your hand out," Good Time explained as he helped get his friend get settled behind a vacant building.

Good Time found Oliver a quiet, safe place to camp outside of an empty, dilapidated office building on a quiet side street. Good Time helped his friend spread his blankets, cardboard, and newspapers for a bed under the overhang. "The building will soon be torn down, but it's adequate for now, Oliver."

He was content to live there, under the shelter, and be dry from the rain.

One late morning that springtime he sensed trouble: he spotted a police car that had stopped across the road nearby.

He tried to sit up, turned his portable radio down, and smoothed out the newspapers that covered his body for warmth.

A female officer slowly opened her door, turned on her flashing lights, and left her partner, the driver, in the cruiser. She soon approached him while he was still dozing from a bad night with arthritic pains in his hips, his knees, and one shoulder.

Oliver rubbed his shoulder and massaged his right hip to quell the pain. "Must be this damn, damp, cool weather," he mumbled to himself.

The officer approached and gently stirred him fully awake with her foot. "What is your name, sir? People are complaining as they walk by, and it is against the law for you to sleep outside with all these paper belongings. Could be a fire hazard," the kindly officer said. She snapped a photo on her iPhone, opened her journal, and began writing.

Oliver pushed the old, moth-eaten blanket off his body and pushed the 'mattress' composed of several old parkas, sweaters, shirts, hordes of newspapers, and plastic sheets off his knees.

He sat up straight and said, looking at her, "I just need a swig of water from my Pepsi Cola bottle, miss. Dry mouth, you can see."

"Yes, I can see that you are parched. Do you need to go to the hospital?"

"God no. I'm well enough. Oliver, my name, missus. So … I'll move soon. Not here long, missus," he answered softly but not very clearly. His eyes blinked and shoulder muscles twitched, but he gave her a decent smile, revealing bad teeth.

"Your full name, please. I see that you have two grocery carts full of clothes, books, and newspapers."

Oliver's eyes almost went into a spasm. He cautiously answered with a slurred tone, fearing she would think it was all stolen. "Yeah … all my personal, like, good stuff. As you can see. So, it's Oliver, missus, Oliver MacKay. My father was a school principal further east. What's your name, missus?" he asked, wanting to be polite.

She smiled back and thought she could just understand what he said with his slurred speech. She was certain that he was sober, safe, and harmless. She diligently continued to make notes.

She stopped writing. "My name? No one ever asks, but its Jasmine. Well, sir, we may have to get a truck and move all your belongings soon. One of our city social counselors will help you move someday. The papers are a fire concern, Mr. MacKay, and this building will come down soon for a high-rise rental."

Oliver just shrugged his shoulders and remained silent. Jasmine just did her job as required, made some more notes, snapped another picture, and left. He lay down and pulled the blanket over him again, worried about her suggestion.

Once she was in her cruiser and gone, he relaxed. It was warming up this day in late May. He peered up at the sun and took his shabby cap off to warm his head.

He knelt down and offered a silent prayer to the small, wooden totem pole statue close by. It was his shrine. It displayed his ancestors, and he prayed to them that he would be left alone from prying do-gooders and the police.

Oliver was homeless, so to speak, but as far as he was concerned he had his home, one where he felt safe, secure, and usually unbothered, even by passersby. Nosey passersby occasionally stopped in his back alley, surveyed his Safeway cart, and dropped some coins in an old, dirty jug he always had beside him.

As time went by, he was only ever bothered occasionally by the police or other do-gooders. Social workers from the city also visited and talked briefly with him, wanting to move him somewhere. "Somewhere that is safe and secure," they always said.

"But greatly bothered, threatened, and abused by those living around me in those grubby hotels," he always replied and told them to go away.

"We have a nice, clean place in a rooming house for you, Oliver. Maybe in a close by hotel," two very young female social workers offered soon after the police officer's third visit. He just waved them away.

Indeed, he was moved once into such a hotel a few years ago.

Just off Hastings and Main Street. It was a decent room, but the place was too noisy for him. Gradually, he became convinced that his neighbor was a drug pusher, that the RCMP were monitoring his every move through the sprinkler system, that the lady down the hall was a big-time hooker, that the desk clerk was an undercover CSIS agent, and that his TV was spying on him throughout the night.

Oliver hated being cramped up in one room. He was nervous, had panic attacks, and was always anxious with his phobic surroundings. He checked out after three weeks and moved back to the streets, where he felt safer: alone and secure.

Carlos, the desk clerk, called out to him as he left, "You're phobic and paranoid. Loony tunes, man. You needs a good shrinker."

Oliver only nodded as he gave Carlos the finger and walked out the door. He brought some of his junk, but left the cans, bottles, and some newspapers in the room for the rats that scurried about. An uneducated man he was, but he silently agreed with Carlos. He knew him to be right with his amateur diagnosis of being a "loony tunes" man.

Oliver never shaved, so looked scruffy with a thin, white, scraggly beard. He always wore the same old, comfortable, ragged jacket with the Toronto Maple Leafs logo up front and old, worn-out jeans. His runners were of different sizes and different makes, which he'd found in a back lane.

He was usually seen in his new neighborhood carrying a black plastic bag on his back, full of whatever, or pushing an old, rusted-out Safeway cart full of more whatevers.

Above him, in the old, rundown, three-story building that he camped beside lived a younger couple. One was an unemployed man with a bad limp and his girlfriend. They, too, lived in a grungy room that he once visited on their invitation to have a coffee.

Oliver was convinced that she was a prostitute, and the man must be with the RCMP, an undercover cop, or most likely with the mafia, since he looked Italian, he thought. After that visit, they avoided him, and he kept away from them.

However, a well-built drug pusher, a brute in his forties called William Sykes, lived with the young ones occasionally. The girl once told Oliver that William was her uncle. He didn't believe her, and he knew for sure that he was her pimp and a drug pusher.

Sykes was a mean bastard, who always wanted Oliver to sell cocaine and heroin to the young people in the nice, upscale neighborhood.

"Them have lots of cash, Oliver," Sykes always said roughly. "I'll give you ten percent." He scowled.

Oliver refused, but was often threatened and pushed around by Sykes, the bully. Sykes also threatened to unleash his ugly bulldog, called Hannibal, on poor Oliver if he didn't help sell drugs. Hannibal was forever tied to Sykes with a heavy chain, but was often let loose when near Oliver. A brute of a dog, he was snarling, slobbering, and always licking his balls.

As his buddy, Good Time, said when he visited occasionally, "Oliver, you've got your head screwed on right; you're smart enough, so stay clear of that motherfucker, Sykes."

Oliver only nodded. Truly, he appeared solitary, slow, and ignorant to those who met him. But he had a good common sense and indeed always had his wits about him.

He was smart enough: he had camped a block away from a large grocery market, where he occasionally bought his food and hustled single women for a few coins. They were the ones who usually had some empathy for him: probably viewing him as a poor, solitary, fatherly figure.

Oliver did have his smarts. He had made arrangements with the bank teller to have his monthly government check, and his aboriginal stipend, deposited into his private account. He also had a bank card so that he could withdraw funds when needed.

Mostly for fun, and to see how they squirmed in guilt, he troubled the clients for some money as they walked out with cash in their pockets after using the ATM.

The visit by Jasmine, the policewoman, was almost a year ago now; he concluded that no one else had complained since he was quiet, never bothered anyone, and was reasonably healthy. Unlike his close buddy, Fast Eddy: a cantankerous young binner and a homeless drug dealer whom he also met outside the bank, manhandling strangers for money.

"So, what happened to my friend, Fast Eddy, and his close lady friend? Ain't seen her much lately, mister officer," Oliver asked the bylaws officer one sunny day. The officer, Fritz, often gave Oliver a few coins as he checked the park periodically for drug pushers hustling or sleeping on the park benches.

Oliver knew that the same bylaws officer often told Fast Eddy and his lady to stop sleeping on the park benches and stop selling drugs to the kids. "Or I'll call the cops on you," he would threaten.

Fritz stopped by and replied sadly, "Mister Eddy's close homeless girlfriend, Matilda, succumbed to an overdose of heroin laced with fentanyl. She died on the park bench near the beach as she lay sleeping one night on his lap, Oliver."

Oliver knew that Sykes had provided Fast Eddy and his girl with heroin. "Poor, stupid Eddy and Matilda, his only good female friend: she and him gave all their monthly social welfare money to Sykes for dope," he told the officer.

"We knew that, but could never catch him pushing," the officer said as he left Oliver at the end of his shift.

Oliver had no other friends nearby and missed Fast Eddy, who was very depressed with his lady's death. Fast Eddy also died of an overdose three weeks after Matilda's demise—on that same park bench.

"It was on that same park bench by the sea, Oliver. Very sad. Very sad, indeed. He missed that nice woman," Fritz, the officer, told Oliver soon after Eddy died.

Oliver was often offered cocaine or heroin by Sykes, who let Hannibal gnaw on Oliver's ankle with each visit. But he refused, and told Sykes, "Buzz off, man, and take your hound with you." He never used drugs, not after seeing what it did to his mother and his friends up north.

He made up for his loss of Eddy by being friendly to those who might stop and talk briefly. Some even threw a few coins into his open jug on the ground beside him, as they chatted.

That was usually when he quietly played on his broken-down, out-of-tune harmonica. He could never carry a tune anyway. The only song he knew was "What a Wonderful World" by Satchmo, which he occasionally heard on his radio.

One day, he again received a visit by that very same policewoman, Jasmine, who was now quite friendly to Oliver. She asked, after some pleasantries, "We know that the man living in this building that you camp under, Sykes, sells drugs to young people, Oliver. We know his name. Many have died of an overdose because of him. It was that killer, fentanyl."

Oliver tensed up and pulled his toque tight over his twitching forehead and tried not to blink rapidly. He finished sipping on his can of soup, which he had heated up on the small, open fire beside him.

He quickly doused the flames with the bottle of Cola next to him and replied fearfully, "So … I keep away from Sykes, missus Jasmine. So … I don't use. I'm clean and don't know him much."

"Many have overdosed, and we've had many who died. Do you know how we can locate him? He's not in the building. My patrolman colleague could only find his bulldog."

"Sorry. Don't know. So … try getting his dog, called Hannibal, to find him. Put him on a leash, and he'll lead you to him," Oliver quietly answered with a smile, praying that would send her away as he shuffled some ragged clothes about in his Safeway cart.

He added as she left, "Hannibal, that dog is vicious. So … be careful."

Oliver didn't wait to hear back from the officer after that anxious conversation. Because of his fear of Sykes and Hannibal, and now the police snooping around, he gathered up his belongings and moved on on a rainy day in August.

Just before he moved, a nice, older lady from Mexico befriended Oliver and told him about an empty house. "Eventually to be torn down, Oliver. But has a nice garden up front," she said as she helped him load his cart.

"It's near the ocean and a park. No one there, Ollie. Nice garden, and I can help you look after it," Rosalina said as she helped him push his cart overloaded with stuff and covered him with her umbrella from the downpour.

Rosalina helped Oliver move in on the dilapidated front steps of that dwelling. He spread out his thin mattress of newspapers, old clothing, and tin cans of soup nearby and settled in. His lady friend showed him what to do with the rose bushes and they both cleaned the area of weeds.

"I have my place to stay, but I'll come and visit, and you can serenade me on your harmonica," Rosalina offered, giggling.

Oliver was camped there for a few months. One evening, after Rosalina had left, the lady officer, Jasmine, returned. "I'm sorry to tell you that we have to move you in the new year, Oliver. The city is demolishing this building, and we have a nice basement room for you close by."

Oliver started twitching again, eyes rolling, and he was scratching his rash on his face that had appeared again. He was able to ask, hoping to divert that fearful suggestion, "Did you find that bulldog and his master, missus?"

The officer, Jasmine, sat down on the steps and waved to her partner, the other patrolman, that she was safe. "Yes, we found him, Mister Sykes. He was in a house close by. The dog led us to him. He had a young girl, dead, in his place. An overdose. He became aggressive and flashed a gun at my partner. Paul, over there," she said.

"My God. What happened? Were you hurt?"

She shook her head. "No, Paul took him down. We had a long history on Sykes. We found his place full of drugs, lots of money, and that dead girl in his bed. You won't be troubled by him anymore, Oliver."

Oliver held his eye from twitching. "The dog? What about Hannibal?"

"Took him to the SPCA. He's okay. The raid was all written up in one of those newspapers that you have rolled up as a pillow," she said and pointed to the papers.

"Thank you for telling me that. I'll read about it someday," Oliver mumbled as he shuffled the papers to find the article.

The nice officer got up to leave. "In a few weeks, we'll bring a truck to take all the belongings that you own and get you a nice warm place. It will be nice and cozy for you." She hesitated for a minute. "You remind me of my father, you know?" she added.

Oliver was surprised by such a personal revelation. He looked up at Jasmine. "Your Pa?"

"Yes, my Pa," she laughed. "My father worked as a detective. Undercover work. He was killed in a raid on a drug house two years ago. Dressed like you. You know, undercover stuff. Nice man."

"Sorry to hear. Sorry," he repeated.

Jasmine was ready to go. "You know, my mother loved that man. She would like you, also."

"She would? Grungy, dirty, smelly, me? Do you think?"

"Sure she would. Grungy, dirty, smelly, you. She would," Jasmine said as she turned away so that Oliver wouldn't see her eyes well up.

Jasmine stopped, dabbed at her tears, and reassured Oliver, "Don't worry, Oliver. We'll take good care of all your worldly possessions when we move you to a nice warm place. All that you own." She waved her hand over all his earthly belongings.

Oliver stood up to stretch as the officer waved goodbye. "It's okay. missus. I, we … that is … all of us … don't really own anything. We're all just passing through this here world," he said as he sat down again.

The officer suddenly stopped. She hesitated for a minute and looked at Oliver. "You know. Funny thing. That's what my father often told my younger brother and me when we were kids. That kinda reminded me, again. Of what my father said."

"Your father said that? I remind you of your father?"

"Yes, Oliver. And my mother, I'm sure, would like you, also," Jasmine repeated and started to walk away again.

With a lump in his throat, Oliver asked again, "Your mother would like me? Really?"

Jasmine walked away to her patrol car, waving goodbye to

Oliver. "You bet she would, Oliver. Mother likes characters like you and she would really like you," she shouted as she got into her car.

HOMELESS CHARACTERS

I included this chapter on homeless men and women because they are often "unseen" by those who pass them by in the alleys, parks, or store fronts. We don't like to see them, avoid them, and always ask, "Why doesn't the city and our government do something about these people?"

I hope that this chapter might try to answer that question, because most, if not all, are troubled personality disorders. They often have some character problems, as did Oliver with mental illness in the above fiction story.

As Oliver explained, he and his buddies had severe anxiety and depression, or schizophrenia or bipolar illness. Most are disordered with character traits including the antisocial, the substance abuse, and the dependent type or the intellectually deprived.

There are many listed online, or you might read about some other well-known homeless people in the newspapers. Charlie

Chaplin was one of them prior to his stage and movie career. WC Fields apparently lived in a hole in a vacant lot, stealing bread and milk from stores, before he became a juggler and then became a comedian.

There is a small, rare group of course, who may be homeless and on the street or living in their cars. They are the ones who are unemployed and can't afford the price of gas or a bus ticket to get home. Some kind of financial assistance, if available, will get them off the street. If they are not drug-dependent, then there is hope for them. Unless they just don't want to work, but if so then they do often suffer from some type of character or personality disorder.

There are some common, understandable reasons for homelessness. They will tell the authorities that they simply do not trust city shelters, or that they simply feel safest on the street due to low visibility. Others are untrusting of any kind of assistance. They fear abuse or thievery in a hostel.

Thousands of mentally ill were previously housed in large psychiatric institutions. When such hospitals closed with the advent of tranquillizers and psychiatric community clinics, many were left out on the streets.

Communities are now increasingly concerned about "tent cities" full of the homeless. Those living in such places do so because they have close, safe friendships with their comrades. For example, the homeless women know their neighbors and usually feel safe from sexual abuse or other forms of harm. Men and women state that they feel that their paltry belongings are safer there. They have a sense of a closer community and are more independent on their own.

Naturally, they are devoid of proper medical, dental, and psychological help. They are exposed to harsh weather conditions and police sweeping the area under orders from the proper authorities.

They are always fearful of losing their belongings, which they have found somewhere and may have an unhealthy attachment to. There are many other obvious obstacles and problems to sleeping in a tent city or elsewhere outdoors, such as in an alley or doorway.

Many of the homeless are basically personality disorders. Some are characters of the antisocial type. This would include hustlers, pimps, and street prostitutes, but also thieves, arsonists, and those addicted to drugs and alcohol. Some are schizoid characters who are very introverted, suspicious, and unrealistic with irrational thoughts.

A large percentage are character disorders who are marginally intellectual by birth. Or they are handicapped due to organic brain disease or head trauma. Many are dependent personality disorders, and some are paranoid characters who believe that others spy on them or want to harm them in some way or another, if placed in a residence (Oliver was such a man, as he explained).

Some of the homeless have been altered in character by early dementia due to Alzheimer's disease (this connotation is a misnomer, since the true Alzheimer's is a pre-senile dementia starting in the early 40's, and death occurs within a few years). Others are the result of trauma to the head, an infectious disease like syphilis, brain tumors, or cardio-vascular disease.

A large percentage of the homeless suffer from schizophrenia or bipolar disorder (previously called manic-depressive disorder). These are not character disorders, but rather are serious mental illnesses. These people were previously housed in long-care psychiatric institutions until such hospitals closed down. Many cities now report these individuals to be the predominant type of homeless people.

Treatment, as in other character disorders already mentioned, is very difficult. The mentally ill require voluntary admission to mental health clinics, out-patient services, or psychiatric wards of general hospitals, but they do not come forward for therapy. Those who do enter therapy are usually diagnosed as mentally ill, offered medication, and then seen on a monthly basis at a clinic. They rarely follow through and rarely comply with the treatment schedule.

Those who are mentally ill and cause a disturbance and brought forth by police or other authorities can be kept in the hospital under legal papers for a short, specified time. Again, follow-up is problematic.

The various types of character disorders can be treated if they have some families, close friends, or community advocates who are supportive and can encourage long-term care. These individuals can respond favorably to ongoing individual or group therapy with a qualified psychologist or counselor.

A family physician can offer appropriate treatment and follow-up if that physician is able to do so. A referral to a psychiatrist may be necessary for psychotherapy or with the use of medication on a prolonged basis.

Once again, compliance is difficult, since they need constant attention and support, almost on a daily basis. Such constant and consistent observation would employ countless numbers of social workers, therapists, aides, nurses, and physicians.

That would be very expensive, but like with Oliver in the above fiction story, perhaps all that is needed for that homeless person is for a caring figure in the neighborhood to say to them, "Yes, Oliver, my father, and my mother, I'm sure, would like you, also."

And as Oliver replied, with a lump in his throat, "Your mother would like me? Really?"

You bet she would, Oliver.

ABOUT THE AUTHOR

Dr. Lawrence E. Matrick received his degree in Medicine from the Manitoba Medical College, and then worked at the Provincial Mental Hospital as a resident in psychiatry. He continued his studies in London, England and received his British degrees in Psychiatry, and later his Fellowship in the Royal College of Physicians, Canada. As an Assistant Professor in Psychiatry at U.B.C., he also had a full-time private practice in Vancouver for almost 50 years. Qualified by the courts, he often attended as an expert witness, dealing with those involved in motor vehicle accidents.